Intimacies

ALSO BY KATIE KITAMURA

Intimacies

KATIE KITAMURA

JONATHAN CAPE
LONDON

3 5 7 9 10 8 6 4

Jonathan Cape, an imprint of Vintage, is part of the Penguin Random House
group of companies whose addresses can be found at
global.penguinrandomhouse.com.

Penguin
Random House
UK

First published by Jonathan Cape in 2021

penguin.co.uk/vintage

A CIP catalogue record for this book is available from the British Library

ISBN 9781787332003

Printed and bound in Great Britain by Clays Ltd, Elcograf S.p.A.

The authorised representative in the EEA is Penguin Random House Ireland,
Morrison Chambers, 32 Nassau Street, Dublin D02 YH68

Penguin Random House is committed to a sustainable future
for our business, our readers and our planet. This book is made
from Forest Stewardship Council® certified paper.

For my family

Intimacies

It is never easy to move to a new country, but in truth I was happy to be away from New York. That city had become disorienting to me, after my father's death and my mother's sudden retreat to Singapore. For the first time, I understood how much my parents had anchored me to this place none of us were from. It was my father's long illness that had kept me there, and with its unhappy resolution I was suddenly free to go. I applied for the position of staff interpreter at the Court on impulse, but once I had accepted the job and moved to The Hague, I realized that I had no intention of returning to New York, I no longer knew how to be at home there.

I arrived in The Hague with a one-year contract at the Court and very little else. In those early days when the city was a stranger to me, I rode the tram without purpose and walked for hours at a time, so that I would sometimes become lost and need to consult the map on my phone. The Hague bore a family resemblance to the European cities in which I had spent long stretches of my life, and perhaps for this reason I was surprised by how easily and frequently I lost my bearings. In those moments, when the familiarity of the streets gave way to confusion, I would wonder if I could be more than a visitor here.

Still, as I traversed the roads and neighborhoods, I had a renewed sense of possibility. I had lived with my slow-moving grief for so long that I had ceased to notice it, or recognize how it blunted my feeling. But now it began to lift. A space opened up. As the days passed I felt that I had been right to leave New York, although I didn't know if I'd been right to come to The Hague. I saw the details of the landscape in high and sometimes startling relief—because the place was not yet worn down by acquaintance or distorted by memory, and because I had begun looking for something, although I didn't know exactly what.

It was around then that I met Jana, through a mutual acquaintance in London. Jana had moved to the Netherlands two years earlier than me, for her job as a curator at the Mauritshuis—the housekeeper of a national gallery, she called the position with a wry shrug. Her character was the opposite of mine, she was almost compulsively open whereas I had grown guarded in recent years—my father's illness had served as a quiet warning against too much hope. She entered my life at a moment when I was more than usually susceptible to the promise of intimacy. I felt a cool relief in her garrulous company, and I thought in our differences we achieved a kind of equilibrium.

Jana and I frequently had dinner together, and that night she had offered to cook, she said she was too tired to eat in a restaurant and it would save us both money, there was the matter of her new and not inconsiderable mortgage. Jana had recently purchased an apartment close to the old train station, and had been urging me to move to the area when the lease on my short-term rental ran out. She had taken to sending me listings, assuring me the neighborhood had much to offer, among other things it was well served for transport, in fact her commute was now easier, a direct tram ride rather than a transfer.

As I walked from the tram stop to her apartment, broken glass crunched underfoot. Jana's building, a modest structure lined with balconies, was wedged between a public housing block and a new condominium of steel and glass, two aspects of a rapidly changing neighborhood. I rang the intercom and she buzzed me in without a word. She opened her door before I was able to knock, things at work were a nightmare, she announced without preamble, she hadn't moved from London to The Hague in order to spend her days poring over Excel spreadsheets. And yet that was exactly how each day passed, she worried over budgets and press releases and as for the art itself, she barely saw any at all, somehow that had become somebody else's responsibility. She waved me in and took the bottle of wine I handed her. Come sit with me while I cook, she called over her shoulder as she disappeared into the kitchen.

I hung up my coat. She handed me a glass of wine as I entered the kitchen and turned back to the stove. The food will be ready in a minute, she said. How was work? Have they said anything about your contract? I shook my head. I didn't know yet whether or not my contract at the Court would be extended. It was something I wondered about with increasing frequency, I had begun to think that I would like to stay in The Hague. I found myself scrutinizing the assignments I received, the manner of my supervisor, seeking an augury of some kind. Jana nodded sympathetically and then asked if I had looked at the listings she had sent, there was an apartment available in the condominium opposite.

I told her I had, then took a sip from the glass of wine. Although she had only recently moved, Jana already appeared at home, she had taken possession of the space with characteristic gusto. I knew that the purchase of the apartment represented a kind of security she had hitherto lacked: she had married and divorced while still in her twenties, and had spent the past decade working her way up to her current position at the Mauritshuis. I watched as she opened the cabinet and took out a bottle of olive oil, a pepper grinder, I noticed that everything already had its place. I felt a throb—not of envy, perhaps of admiration, although the two are not unrelated.

Shall we eat at the counter? Jana asked. I nodded and sat down. She set a bowl of pasta before me and then said, I always wanted a kitchen with an eating counter. It must have been something I saw as a child. She sat down on the stool beside me. Jana had grown up in Belgrade with a Serbian mother and Ethiopian father, before being sent to a boarding school in France during the war. She never returned to Yugoslavia, or what was now called former Yugoslavia. I wondered where she had seen her first eating counter, the one that she had at last succeeded in replicating in some form, here in this kitchen.

I congratulated her on the aspiration fulfilled and she smiled. It does feel good, she said. It wasn't easy, the process of finding the apartment, and then getting the financing— she shook her head and gave me a droll look. It turns out it's not easy getting a mortgage as a single Black woman in your forties. She reached for her glass of wine. Of course, I am a gentrifier here. But I have to live somewhere—

At that moment the sound of a siren erupted in the street. I looked up, startled. The sound grew louder and then ballooned inside the apartment as the vehicle approached. Red and orange light spiraled through the kitchen. Jana frowned.

Outside, the sound of doors slamming and the low rumble of an engine. There are police here all the time, she said as she reached for her glass of wine. There have been a couple muggings, there was a shooting last year. I don't feel unsafe, she added quickly. Even as she spoke, another pair of sirens drew near. Jana picked up her fork and continued eating. I watched as she chewed slowly, the choral sound outside growing louder. It's no different to the London neighborhoods I used to live in, Jana said. She raised her voice in order to be heard over the noise. It's just that living in The Hague inures you. It can be easy to forget what being in a real city is like.

The sirens cut out and we sat in the sudden silence. A siren can mean anything, I said at last. A slip in the bath, a heart attack in the kitchen. She nodded and I realized her apprehension was not caused by the threat of danger or violence, or not that alone—it was that her sense of the apartment had mutated. In that moment, it was no longer a source of the security she had long sought but something else altogether, something more changeable, and uncertain.

The remainder of the evening passed under a cloud of preoccupation, and before too long I said that I would be going. I went into the living room to collect my things, as I pulled on my coat I peered through the curtains at the street below, now dimly lit by streetlamps. The road was still, apart from the glow of a cigarette—a man walking his dog. As I watched, he threw the cigarette to the ground and tugged on the dog's leash before disappearing around the corner.

Jana leaned against the wall, she had a cup of tea in one hand and she looked more than usually tired. I smiled at her. Get some rest, I said, and she nodded. She opened the front door and as I moved past she suddenly caught me by the arm. Be careful on your way to the tram, will you? I was surprised by the urgency in her voice, the grip of her fingers on my arm. She let go and took a step back. It's just you can't be too cautious, she said. I nodded and turned to go, she had already closed the door behind me. I heard the click of one lock turning, and then another, and then silence.

2.

I lived in the city center, in a very different neighborhood to Jana's. Prior to my arrival, I had found my furnished apartment by way of online listings. The Hague was not a cheap city to live in, but it was cheaper than New York. As a result, I lived in an apartment that was too big for one person, with two bedrooms and separate dining and living rooms.

It took me some time to grow accustomed to the size of the apartment, an effect exacerbated by the furnishings, which were somehow too perfunctory for its proportions. A foldout futon in the living room, a compact dinette in the dining room, the space was designed to be both temporary and impersonal. When I signed the lease I had considered that vacancy a luxury, I remember walking through the apartment, my footsteps hollow, marking one room the bedroom, another a possible study. In time that feeling faded, and the dimensions of the apartment no longer seemed remarkable. Nor did the interim nature of the accommodation, although when I returned that evening from Jana's, I recalled the ease with which she'd seemed to inhabit her apartment, and felt a ripple of vague longing.

When I woke the next morning it was still dark outside. I made a coffee and pulled on a coat and went out onto the balcony—another feature of the apartment, one that I used even during these frigid winter months. I had wedged a small table and a single folding chair against the wall, along with a few potted plants, now withered. I sat down. It was early enough that the streets below were empty. The Hague was a quiet city, and almost strenuously civilized. But the more time I spent there, the more its air of courtesy, the preserved buildings and manicured parks, imparted a sense of unease. I recalled what Jana had said about living in The Hague, how it inured you to what a real city was like. This was possibly true, increasingly I'd begun to think the docile surface of the city concealed a more complex and contradictory nature.

Only last week, I had been shopping in the Old Town when I saw three uniformed men moving down the busy pedestrian street alongside a large machine. Two of the men held slender picks while the third held a large nozzle that protruded from the machine, the effect was rather as if he were leading an elephant by the trunk. I had paused to observe them without really knowing why, perhaps only because I wondered what manner of slow-moving work they were doing.

They eventually approached and I could see exactly the task they were performing, the two men with the picks were carefully extracting cigarette butts from between the cracks of the cobbled road, one by one by one, painstaking labor that explained their sluggish pace of progress. I looked down and realized that the road was strewn with cigarette butts, this despite the fact that there were several well-placed public ashtrays on that stretch of street alone. The two men continued to flip the cigarette butts out of the cracks while the third man followed with his elephantine vacuum, dutifully sucking up the debris with the machine, the drum of which presumably held many thousands or even hundreds of thousands of cigarette butts, each of which had been disappeared from the street by the work of these men.

The three men were almost certainly immigrants, possibly Turkish and Surinamese. Meanwhile, their labor was necessitated by the heritage aesthetic of the city, not to mention the carelessness of a wealthy population that dropped its cigarette butts onto the pavement without a thought, when the designated receptacle was only a few feet away, I now saw that there were dozens of cigarette butts on the ground directly below the ashtrays. It was only an anecdote. But it was one example of how the city's veneer of civility was constantly giving way, in places it was barely there at all.

Around me the light was beginning to come up, color blotting the horizon. I went inside and dressed for work. I left the apartment not long after, I was now running late. I hurried to the nearby tram stop. Jana called me while I was waiting, she was still at home and I could hear her moving through the apartment, collecting her keys and gathering her books and papers. She asked if I had made it home safely and I assured her that the journey had passed without incident. There was a pause, I heard the slam of a door, she was on her way out of her building and into the street. She sounded distracted, almost as if she could not remember why she had called, then she reminded me that I was bringing Adriaan to her house for dinner on Saturday, and asked if there was anything in particular he did or did not eat.

The tram was arriving and I told her that anything would be fine, and that I would call her later. I hung up and boarded the tram and was soon jolting toward the Court, where I was now nearly six months into my contract. Most of my colleagues had lived in multiple countries and were cosmopolitan in nature, their identity indivisible from their linguistic capabilities. I qualified in much the same way. I had native fluency in English and Japanese from my parents, and in French from a childhood in Paris. I had also studied Spanish and German to the point of professional proficiency, although these along with Japanese were less essential than English and French, the working languages of the Court.

But fluency was merely the foundation for any kind of interpretive work, which demanded extreme precision, and I often thought that it was my natural inclination toward the latter, rather than any linguistic aptitude, that made me a good interpreter. That exactitude was even more important in a legal context, and within a week of working at the Court I learned that its vocabulary was both specific and arcane, with official terminology that was set in each language, and then closely followed by all the interpreters on the team. This was done for obvious reasons, there were great chasms beneath words, between two or sometimes more languages, that could open up without warning.

As interpreters it was our job to throw down planks across these gaps. That navigation—which alongside accuracy required a certain amount of native spontaneity, at times you had to improvise in order to rapidly parse a difficult phrase, you were always working against the clock—was more significant than you might initially think. With inconsistent interpretation, for example, a reliable witness could appear unreliable, seeming to change his or her testimony with each new interpreter. This in turn could affect the outcome of a trial, the judges were unlikely to note a change of personnel in the interpreters' booth, even if the voice speaking in their ears suddenly became markedly different, switching from male to female, from halting to deliberate.

They would only note the change in their perception of the witness. A sliver of unreliability introducing fractures into the testimony of the witness, those fractures would develop into cracks, which would in turn threaten the witness's entire persona. Every person who took to the stand was projecting an image of one kind or another: their testimony was heavily coached and shaped by either the defense or the prosecution, they had been brought to the Court in order to perform a role. The Court was run according to the suspension of disbelief: every person in the courtroom knew but also did not know that there was a great deal of artifice surrounding matters that were nonetheless predicated on authenticity.

In the Court, what was at stake was nothing less than the suffering of thousands of people, and in suffering there could be no question of pretense. And yet the Court was by nature a place of high theatrics. It was not only in the carefully crafted testimony of the victims. The first time I at-

tended a session I had been startled, both the prosecution
and the defense had been unmeasured in pleading their cases.
And then the accused themselves were often grandiose in
character, both imperious and self-pitying, they were politi-
cians and generals, people used to occupying a large stage
and hearing the sound of their own voices. The interpreters
couldn't entirely eschew these dramatics, it was our job not
only to interpret the words the subject was speaking, but
also to express or indicate the demeanor, the nuance and intention behind their words.

The first time you listened to an interpreter speaking,
their voice might sound cold and precise and completely
without inflection, but the longer you listened, the more
variation you would hear. If a joke was made it was the interpreter's job to communicate the humor or attempt at humor; similarly, when something was said ironically it was
important to indicate that the words were not to be taken at
face value. Linguistic accuracy was not enough. Interpretation was a matter of great subtlety, a word with many con-
texts, for example it is often said that an actor interprets a
role, or a musician a piece of music.

There was a certain level of tension that was intrinsic to
the Court and its activities, a contradiction between the intimate nature of pain, and the public arena in which it had
to be exhibited. A trial was a complex calculus of performance in which we were all involved, and from which none

15

of us could be entirely exempt. It was the job of the interpreter not simply to state or perform but to repeat the unspeakable. Perhaps that was the real anxiety within the Court, and among the interpreters. The fact that our daily activity hinged on the repeated description—description, elaboration, and delineation—of matters that were, outside, generally subject to euphemism and elision.

The tram was crowded, and at one point a large group of students boarded. They were raucous, but unlike some of the other passengers—who glanced at them askance before looking away—I did not mind, on the contrary I took the opportunity to listen to their conversation, or at least what fragments I could decipher.

When I moved to The Hague I did not speak or have more than a passing acquaintance with Dutch, however its similarities with German were such that after six months I had some competence in the language. Of course, most people in the Netherlands spoke fluent English, and at the Court there was never an occasion to speak Dutch, so I primarily learned through listening—in the street, in a restaurant or café, on the tram as I was doing now. A place has a curious quality when you have only a partial understanding of its language, and in those early months the sensation was especially peculiar. At first I moved in a cloud of unknowing, the speech around me impenetrable, but it quickly grew less elusive as I began to understand single words and then phrases and now even snippets of conversation. On occasion, I found myself stumbling into situations more intimate than I would have liked, the city was no longer the innocent place it had been when I arrived.

But there was nothing essentially invasive about listening here on the tram, the students were speaking loudly, almost at the top of their lungs, they intended to be overheard. As I listened to them, I was reminded of the pleasure of learning a new language, unlocking its systems, testing their give and flexibility. It had been some time since I had experienced this particular feeling, having acquired all my other languages as a child or later in school. The students were speaking a Dutch peppered with slang, making it difficult for me to understand exactly what they were saying, mostly they seemed to be talking about school, some teacher or friend who was irritating them.

Two or three tram stops later, I thought I heard one of the girls say *verkrachting*, the Dutch word for rape. I looked up, startled, my mind had started to drift and I was no longer following their conversation as closely as I had been when I boarded. The girl who spoke was perhaps twelve or thirteen years old, her eyes were rimmed with heavy liner and she had a nose piercing. She continued speaking, I heard the phrase *bel de politie*, or I thought I did. But then the girl she was speaking to began giggling in response and after a moment the girl with the nose piercing also began to laugh and I was no longer certain of what I had heard, after all rape and calling the police were not exactly a laughing matter. The girl with the nose piercing must have felt my gaze, abruptly she turned and stared at me, and although she was still laughing her eyes were hard and empty, entirely mirthless.

The tram approached my stop. The girls were now discussing a new sneaker brand, and although I glanced several more times at the girl, she ignored me. Unsettled by the encounter, I disembarked. The tram moved away and then the Court stood directly before me, a large glass complex that was nestled into the dunes on the edge of the city. It was easy to forget that The Hague was situated on the North Sea, in so many ways it was a city that seemed to face inward, its back turned against the open water.

Prior to my arrival, when I had applied for and then was offered the position, the Court had existed in my mind as a near medieval institution, in the manner of the Binnenhof, the Parliament complex only a couple miles away in the center of the city. Even after I arrived and for the first month of my employment, I had been startled every time I encountered the building. I knew very well that the Court was a recent invention, having been founded only a decade earlier, but the modern architecture still seemed incongruous, perhaps even lacking the authority I had expected.

Six months later, it was merely the place of my employment: everything grows normal after a time. I greeted the guards as I entered and passed through the detector—a question or two about their families, some statement about the weather, it was on these occasions that I could practice my Dutch. I collected my bag and proceeded across the courtyard and into the building. There I saw Robert, another interpreter at the Court, who waited for me to join him. He was a large and affable Englishman, outgoing and charming; in my relative reticence I was unusual among interpreters. If interpretation is a kind of performance, then its practitioners tend to be confident and garrulous. Robert exemplified these characteristics, he played rugby on the weekends and took part in amateur theater productions. We were never paired together in the booth, but I sometimes wondered what manner of partner he would make, it would be hard not to feel upstaged by his presence, not to attempt to match the cadences and flourishes of his voice, which was unusually mellifluous, the product of his class and a childhood spent in English boarding schools.

As we made our way up to the office, Robert informed me that none of the chambers would be in session that day, which was frankly a relief, he assumed I was as far behind in paperwork as he was. We greeted our colleagues as we made our way to our desks, the interpreters worked in a single open-plan space, with the exception of the head, Bettina, who had her own office. There was a distinctly collegial atmosphere within the department, due in part to the fact that most of the team had come to the Netherlands in order to work at the Court, having amassed the requisite body of experience elsewhere. Some were like me and did not know how long they would remain either at the Court or in the Netherlands, while others had more or less settled here, Amina for example had recently married a Dutch man and was pregnant.

Now she sat at her desk, her face serene as she reviewed the documents before her. While most interpreters could on occasion become flustered or even exasperated, in some cases requesting that a witness slow down, Amina was always composed, she was able to interpret with a consistency and speed that was remarkable, whatever the circumstances. As she approached the latter stages of the pregnancy, she was if anything even more unflappable, her manner was perpetually calm. While the rest of us would struggle with foibles in speech or delivery, Amina alone never seemed to experience difficulty.

But such praise made her uncomfortable, and Amina frequently insisted that she was far from faultless. As I sat down at my desk, I recalled an anecdote she had told me not long after I arrived at the Court. It was a story I thought of often. She had been tasked with interpreting for the accused, working in Swahili, and was briefly the only interpreter on the team with adequate fluency to perform the task. Her booth partner did not have a strong grasp on the language, and said in private that her mind had drifted during the lengthy sessions, she listened to the originating English and French but less closely to Amina's interpretation.

But while her partner might have found the days less than taxing, Amina herself was under considerable pressure, she was negotiating marathon sessions that were far longer than standard. She sat in the mezzanine-level booth, the accused positioned directly below her in the courtroom. He was still a young man, a former militia leader, wearing an expensive suit and slouched in an ergonomically designed office chair. He was on trial for hideous crimes and yet he simply looked, as he sat, sullen and perhaps a little bored. Of course, the accused are often in suits and in office chairs, but the difference lay in the fact that at the Court the accused were not mere criminals who had been dressed up for the occasion, but men who had long worn the mantle of authority conveyed by a suit or uniform, men who were accustomed to its power.

And they had a kind of magnetism, in part innate and in

part heightened by the circumstances. The Court was generally unable to bring the accused into custody without the cooperation of foreign governments or bodies, and its powers of arrest were fairly limited. There were many outstanding warrants, and many accused being held in other countries, it was not as if we had a plethora of war criminals in our midst. The accused therefore had an aura when they were brought to The Hague, we had heard a great deal about these men (and they were almost always men), we had seen photographs and video footage and when they finally appeared in the Court they were the stars of the show, there was no other way of putting it, the situation staged their charisma.

In the case of this particular man, he was not only young and undeniably handsome—many of the men on trial were elderly, far past their prime, compelling but not in and of themselves physically impressive—but he had a dazzling air of command, even without the aid of the courtroom, it was easy to see why and how so many people had obeyed his orders. But it was not even this, Amina explained, it was the intimacy of the interpretation, she was interpreting for one man and one man alone, and when she spoke into the microphone, she was speaking to him. Of course, she had known when she accepted the post in The Hague that the substance of the Court would be darker than the United Nations, where she had previously been working. After all, the Court concerned itself exclusively with genocide, crimes against humanity, war crimes. But she had not expected this kind of proximity: although she was never face-to-face with the accused and was always safely ensconced behind the glass-fronted interpreters' booth, she was constantly aware that she and the accused were the only two people in the courtroom who understood the language she was speaking, his own counsel was made up of English barristers with no knowledge of either French or their client's native tongue.

Over the course of these first sessions, Amina grew increasingly uneasy. The case involved a great deal of testimony regarding terrible atrocities, and hour by hour she carried this testimony from one language into another. She found herself on occasion struggling to control the tremor in her voice, she felt herself becoming entirely too emotional. But then, as quickly as the second day and for reasons she did not fully understand, a certain hardness overtook her, she discovered a new and acerbic tone, not exactly neutral, perhaps even reproachful. At one point, as she relayed the details of an embezzlement scheme, something that was morally questionable but a trifle compared to the other charges against the man, she found herself using a voice of cold disapproval, as if she were a wife scolding a husband for some small domestic failing, neglecting to do the dishes, for example, rather than addressing his rampant infidelity, or the fact that he had gambled away their life's savings.

At that moment, to her surprise, she saw the accused turn his head and look up in the direction of the interpreters. Until this point, he had sat almost entirely still, staring straight ahead, as if the proceedings had nothing to do with him, as if the entire matter was beneath him, although the result, Amina thought, was not the appearance of dignity; rather, he looked like a sulky teenager being reprimanded for some infraction for which he refused to repent. There were perhaps half a dozen interpreters seated in the mezzanine-level booths, it was unlikely that he would know which one of them was his, she had never before noted him observing them. She forced herself to keep her voice steady and focus on the job at hand, the last thing she wanted to do was get distracted. Nonetheless, she was unable to keep from surreptitiously watching the accused, as his gaze swept the glass-fronted booths.

Perhaps feeling her eyes upon him, he suddenly stopped and looked directly at her, turning in his chair in order to do so. Amina couldn't help it, she stumbled over her words, apologized, nearly lost the thread of what was being said. He continued to stare at her, a grim expression of satisfaction settling into his handsome face, perhaps because he had succeeded in intimidating her, in causing her to falter. She felt at once, even through the glass wall dividing them, the totality of the man's will. She shivered and looked down.

She resumed interpreting, scribbling on her pad, as if making notes. When she looked up again, he had turned and was looking straight ahead once more, his face soft and brooding.

He never looked at her again. However, she found that her voice had shifted, despite herself she had been cowed. The next time she was required to recite a litany of the horrific acts perpetrated by the accused, her voice took on a pleading tone, in response to which the accused gave a thin smile. Somehow, she had become uncomfortable with the idea of confronting the man with his crimes, these heinous accusations that she was not herself making but was simply interpreting on behalf of the Court. Don't shoot the messenger, she almost added, before remembering that this was precisely the kind of thing the accused did, it might even have been on the list of crimes, actually shooting the messenger. Although she knew there was nothing the man could do to her, she could not deny that she was afraid, he was a man who inspired fear, even while sitting immobile he radiated power.

Still, it was not primarily fear that she felt, but guilt. She felt guilty toward the accused, who not only was a terrible man, but a man for whom she bore no responsibility, apart from adequately interpreting what was said in the courtroom, and doing her part to ensure that he received a fair trial. She bore no responsibility for his happiness, she doubted that the man had been happy since he had been taken into custody by the Court. He was a man entirely without morals, and yet the sentiment she felt toward him was moral in nature. It was illogical, it didn't make any sense. She concluded that it was the man's magnetism, which had persuaded thousands of people to commit terrible acts of violence; again there was nothing bureaucratic or banal about him. He was a leader in every sense of the word, she thought as she leaned toward the microphone and continued to interpret, steadily and without pause. He did not turn to look at her, he never did again, after that instance. But it was, she thought in retrospect, her first true encounter with evil.

The day passed uneventfully enough, and soon it was early evening and I was leaving the Court. It was raining, and as I peered up at the sky and unfolded my umbrella, my phone rang. It was Jana again. Almost before I could speak, she told me that she had just arrived at her building. There's police tape, she said.

The rain was loud on the umbrella, almost deafening, and it was difficult to hear. Someone else was calling. I lowered the phone and saw Adriaan's name. The rain was falling harder now. I lifted the phone back to my ear as it continued to pulse.

What do you mean?

On the side street, the passageway. Do you know the one? I often take it from the tram. It's been blocked with police tape. Something must have happened last night.

The phone was still ringing. Jana, I said, I have another call—

There's no signs or anything. But the passageway is closed off.

In my hand, the phone had stopped vibrating.

Jana—

I'll call you later.

She hung up, and before I could lower the phone, it buzzed again, a message telling me that I had one missed call followed by a second message, from Adriaan, saying that he would be ten minutes late to meet me, and apologizing in advance.

3.

I met Adriaan at a restaurant in the city center. Despite having warned me that he would be late, he was waiting at the table when I arrived. Before moving to The Hague, I had not associated punctuality with the Dutch character, but Adriaan in particular was incapable of tardiness. He stood when he saw me, I thought again that he was very handsome, and I felt a sense of happy surprise, that this was the man I was meeting for dinner.

Adriaan was the reason why I wanted to stay in The Hague, or at least one of the reasons, though I was embarrassed to admit this even to myself—I did not like to think of myself as a woman who made decisions in this way, for a man. Particularly when things were still so nascent, and the situation so complicated. We had met only four months earlier, but there was already a certain amount of routine to the way we were together. That regularity had many possible meanings and was difficult to interpret, at times I thought it was the expression of an intrinsic ease between us, some deep familiarity superseding our many differences. But at other times it seemed it was a product of habit, and that he knew no other way of being with a woman.

"Habit" because Adriaan was married with children, although the situation was at once less stark and more difficult than it sounded. He had been left by his wife a year earlier. She had left him for another man, with whom she was now comfortably ensconced, not in The Hague or Rotterdam or Amsterdam even, but in Lisbon. She had left the country altogether, removing herself from the bad weather and the marriage and sending for the children one month after she had gone. The children, who had been neither taken nor left by her, the arrangement was not entirely clear, not even now, one year later.

I had learned this not long after we had first met. I had gone with Adriaan to a party. We were at the stage when nothing had been declared between us, and when he introduced me to people at the party there was no purpose behind the introduction, I was not yet his "girlfriend" or "date" or even necessarily someone he was sleeping with. Perhaps because of that apparent neutrality, it did not seem especially awkward or significant when a man—not unattractive, of a similar age and general disposition to Adriaan,

not as handsome but entirely presentable, so that I was by
no means displeased when I saw him approaching—drew
me aside and asked how long I had known Adriaan.

The question did not sound loaded, presumably he had
seen us arrive together. Not very long, I replied. He nodded, as if he had expected this answer. I wondered then
if Adriaan regularly turned up to parties with different
women, none of whom endured for a second outing, I knew
relatively little about him at the time. We were standing on
a bridge suspended across a large atrium, which was full of
stylish and glamorous people, it was the launch of a city-
wide cultural fund. Below, waiters circulated through the
crowd serving canapés executed with outlandish precision.
My eyes followed a waiter as he weaved across the atrium
carrying a tray of miniature grilled cheese sandwiches,
pausing as party guests plucked up the carefully charred tri-
angles. He passed a tall man, I realized after a moment that
it was Adriaan.

Very surprising what happened, the man standing beside me said. I nodded, distracted, as if I knew what he was
talking about. Adriaan was deep in conversation with a
woman whose back was turned toward me. As I watched,
she waved her hand through the air, Adriaan leaned closer
as if he had not quite heard the words she had spoken. His
handsome face bowed down to hers. A moment later, she
laughed, tossing her head back to reveal her throat.

I knew her quite well, he said. I looked up at the man beside me, he had put a great deal of product in his hair, so that it stood up in rigid and glistening waves. He obviously wished to emphasize the plenitude of his tresses, at his age many men had already begun to lose some or all of their hair, but the effect was a little absurd, he looked not like a virile man in the prime of his life but rather like a juvenile and inexperienced teenaged boy who had not yet learned how to manage his appearance. They were a bit of a golden couple, he continued. I think they even met at university, over the years they grew to resemble each other—both very tall, both very good-looking, eventually both successful and sophisticated. It just goes to show, the man said, a sneer crossing his near handsome face, how little you know of what really happens inside a marriage.

The utterance was entirely commonplace but I was startled, at that point I did not even know that Adriaan was or had been married. I turned to look at the man, who was gratified either by the small attention or my expression of surprise and smiled smugly. Even from the inside, he continued, encouraged, what do you really know of your own marriage? One day you realize you are living with a stranger. It must have been like that for Adriaan, she left in such a horrible way, she went away to Lisbon for the weekend and never came back. He didn't even know what to tell the children, whether or not she would be returning, they are teenagers, the worst possible age for something like that to happen.

I nodded, I said mechanically that adolescence was difficult enough without that kind of an interruption, one could only imagine their reaction to such a betrayal. Apparently she sent Adriaan an email, the man continued. One would have expected a call at the very least, don't you think? And I had to agree, there was something cruel about sending an email, it was too convenient a mode of communication for a matter so grave, you could tell she was a selfish and self-absorbed person. Still, Gaby has always been very honest with Adriaan, the man said, and that's something, isn't it?

When did this happen? I asked. The man shrugged. Less than a year ago. She left in the dead of winter, perhaps she'd had enough of the bad weather. I looked through the glass sides of the atrium, that night too, rain was falling. I took out my phone and looked up the weather in Lisbon: a balmy 70 degrees and sunny. The man self-consciously touched his lustrous hair before asking if I wanted another drink. Below us, Adriaan was still speaking to the woman. She must have said something amusing because Adriaan laughed, his eyes still on her, even from a distance I could see that he was interested in this woman. I was suddenly gripped by the definite sensation that he would leave the party with her, having arrived with me, the feeling so vivid it was like a premonition. The woman turned, she set her glass on the tray of a passing waiter. For a fleeting moment I saw her profile, she had small but pronounced features, a face full of clarity. Winter in Lisbon is meant to be wonderful, the man said,

I excused myself, I could bear his presence no longer. The man seemed surprised, perhaps he thought he'd been making some headway with me. I crossed the bridge and descended the stairs, rejoining the party below. I made my way toward Adriaan, he looked up, immediately he stretched his arm out to stop me. Where have you been, he asked, and he turned to the woman he had been speaking with. She put her hand out and introduced herself, her manner friendly and perhaps a little curious, as we spoke Adriaan casually placed his hand at the back of my neck. She moved away soon after, almost without leaving an impression, as Adriaan turned to me it seemed odd that I had been so threatened by this woman, someone clearly of minimal significance to him, and with whom he had only been making small talk.

But I had also only been making small talk with the man on the bridge, I had been away from Adriaan for no more than ten or perhaps twenty minutes. Nonetheless, in that brief span of time he had been transformed, I looked at him and his handsome exterior, he in no way seemed like a figure unmanned, someone nursing a private wound. And yet he had been abandoned by his wife in the cruelest and most humiliating manner, he was now a figure to be whispered over at parties, a man whose most intimate catastrophe was now the stuff of idle and malicious gossip. He looked around the party, his manner was a little restless, and as I watched him, contours appeared to his face that I had been unable to see before, for better or worse, he was now a more complicated figure in my imagination.

He asked if I wanted to get some fresh air, and said he wanted a cigarette, sadly he had started smoking again. He was not looking at me as he spoke and I did not ask what had caused this resumption of a habit that, from his expression, he had clearly struggled to lose. He took my elbow and steered me toward one of the many covered balconies that lined the atrium. The rain had not slackened and the balcony was empty. Adriaan took out a cigarette, he was about to light it when the glass door to the balcony opened again, and the man from the bridge emerged. Adriaan looked up, he did not immediately greet the man, although it was obvious that he recognized him. I thought that was you slipping away with the young lady, the man said. Adriaan did not reply. He played with the cigarette between his fingers for a moment longer and then slipped it into the breast pocket of his suit jacket as if to save it for later, perhaps he did not want to be seen smoking in front of this man.

Adriaan remained silent as he regarded the man from

the bridge, who now appeared a little nonplussed, despite the aggression of his own greeting he was clearly taken aback by the coldness of Adriaan's reply. Do you two know each other? Adriaan asked at last. His manner was casual, I could see from the way he spoke that he made no presumption of prior acquaintance, it was more that he wished to downplay the introduction, as much to say, *This is not a man worth knowing, not a person who warrants a formal introduction.*

The man gave a wolfish grin. To my horror, he reached out and wrapped his arm around my waist. We're the best of friends, he said. He did not look at me but trained his gaze on Adriaan, who suddenly reached into the pocket of his jacket and took out the cigarette after all. The man's touch was damp and somehow sticky, even through the layers of my clothing. It wasn't the nature of his skin, whether or not his palms or fingers were perspiring, but rather the quality of his grip around my waist that gave this impression; it was like being embraced by a squid or an octopus, a cephalopod of some kind.

Adriaan lifted the cigarette to his lips, he regarded us with an expression that was suddenly wary, his eyes hooded, perhaps he imagined that the man was an old boyfriend of mine, although at that point I had barely been in The Hague long enough for such a thing to be possible. More plausible was the possibility that we had shared a casual sexual encounter, one or two nights together, I could easily imagine that the man's sexual record was made up almost exclusively of such minor events. The man gripped harder, his arm tight around my waist and his thumb now rubbing at the waistband of my stockings through the fabric of my skirt, the slow and regular movement both lewd and gratuitous, he was virtually a stranger to me, I didn't even know his name. Adriaan lowered his head to light the cigarette and I pulled myself away. We spoke up on the bridge just now, I said, I got lost looking for the bathroom.

Adriaan exhaled, a wreath of smoke rising up around his face. He waved his hand as if to clear it. I don't even know your name, I said to the man, I don't think you introduced yourself, you said only that you were a friend of Adriaan's. The man frowned, he had shoved his hands into his pockets when I moved away and now looked even more like a petulant teenager, like someone who had been caught in the act. Adriaan was watching him, he did not say anything and the man did not introduce himself to me either. I was a friend of Gaby's, the handsome man said at last, Or rather, I was a friend of Gaby's first.

Adriaan still did not say anything, he was not looking at me, in that moment it was as if I were not present at all, not only to Adriaan but also to the man, who had turned to meet Adriaan's gaze. The two men stared at each other, I understood then that there was some history of animosity between them, that the man had not approached me for myself, but rather because of my connection to Adriaan. What he perceived that connection to be, I did not know. A friend? Adriaan said, after a considerable pause, Yes, I suppose that is one way of putting it. The man grew flushed beneath his lacquered hair, he looked uneasy, as if he had not expected so direct a response. A long time ago, he said lamely, Gaby and I have known each other since we were children.

You've spoken to her lately? Adriaan asked, or at least I thought he asked. It was difficult to tell from his voice whether it was a question or a statement, but in any case I understood that it was a loaded and possibly aggressive thing to say. The man grew even more flushed, he looked over his shoulder and back to the party with longing, he must have been thinking that it had been a mistake to come out onto the balcony. When he joined us he'd had the air of a man who had the upper hand, or believed himself to, but now he simply looked as if he were wondering how quickly he would be able to extricate himself from the situation.

Adriaan now turned to me, Kees is a good friend of my wife's. That was the first time he had mentioned Gaby, or the fact that he was, that he had been, married. The truth is, he continued, they were lovers before Gaby and I were married, and although that was many years ago they remained very close, very close indeed, during the years of our marriage. I blinked at the phrase *very close, very close indeed*, the insinuation was crude and out of character. Adriaan continued, I am sure that Kees is in touch with Gaby at this very moment. As for me, I know next to nothing of what she is doing, of what she is thinking, or even exactly where she is.

Please, Adriaan, the man interrupted, his hands fluttering up to his hair. I am entirely on your side in the matter, I haven't spoken to Gaby in months, not since she left. She sends me the occasional email here and there but nothing of significance, I promise you.

Adriaan stared at him a moment before turning back to me. The two of them were on the phone together almost every night, he continued relentlessly. He was now almost loquacious, he spoke to me as if I were familiar with all the details of his marriage when in reality he had told me nothing, not until that moment, not the fact that he had a wife, not even the fact that he had children. I understood well enough that Adriaan was not speaking to me but to Kees, that I was only the medium through which his statements were passing, and similarly I understood that my presence must have been what allowed Adriaan to speak so directly to Kees, it was as if he were saying things he had wished to say for many years but had been unable to, perhaps restrained by the basic courtesies of marriage, his respect for the long-standing friendship between his wife and this man.

Simply a confidant, Kees said weakly, and really against my will. She always called me, it was always at her instigation, I never called except in response to a message or a missed call. Why me rather than one of her many girlfriends I've no idea. And this was at all hours of day and night, I assure you I didn't enjoy the intimacy, it was sometimes rather annoying, I have my own share of personal troubles, as you know. He made a gesture of appeal to Adriaan, who remained stony-faced, although I did not doubt that he knew more than he cared to about the man's trials and tribulations, probably Kees had been a frequent dinner guest at their household, back when it had been a household, the couple's regular bachelor friend.

Gaby was never very sensitive, Kees said and looked at Adriaan with a little shrug, as if to say, You of course would be the first to know that. But during those months it became truly astonishing, it became so that I would not take her phone calls unless I had the evening clear, a good hour or two, sometimes more, it was impossible to get her to stop talking, even if you said my friend has just arrived or I have a deadline, she was deaf to such excuses, she could not accept the possibility of there being anything or anyone more interesting than her and her troubles. Of course, Gaby was very used to people listening to her, whatever her faults, you must admit that she was—or rather she is, because it is not as if she has died, she is still with us—a fascinating woman.

Gaby has always been herself, Adriaan said irritably. Kees stared at him for a moment and then nodded, obviously on this point there could be no disagreement. He then excused himself, there seemed to be nothing else to say. Adriaan gave him a curt nod as he smoked another cigarette. We left the party shortly after. You would not necessarily think it, Adriaan said as we walked to his car, but Kees is a very successful defense lawyer, one of the best in the country.

I said that I could see that, he had the moral flexibility that I thought was surely common to many defense lawyers. Adriaan shook his head. In the end, I am not so sure it has to do with moral flexibility, he said, certainly less than appears at first glance. Everyone deserves fair legal representation, even the most depraved criminal, even someone who has performed unspeakable crimes, the kind of acts that defy the imagination, the mere description of which would make most of us cover our ears and turn away. The defense lawyer does not have recourse to such cowardice, he or she must not only listen to but carefully study the record of these acts, he or she must inhabit and inhale their atmosphere. The very thing that the rest of us are unable to endure is the very thing inside of which the defense lawyer must live.

He frowned. And yet, Kees is petty and essentially frivolous as a person, it is one of those paradoxes of personality or nature. I nodded, and we walked in silence for a time.

When we reached his car, I stopped and turned to face him. The street was empty and the rain had cleared. You're married, I said.

Yes, he said at once. But I don't know for how much longer. Is that okay?

The words themselves were simple to the point of being blunt, but they were also words that did not try to deflect or avoid. I could have walked away then, and chosen not to involve myself any further. But I was disarmed by his honesty, by the simple question that was so difficult to answer. The appearance of simplicity is not the same thing as simplicity itself, even then I was aware of this. As if conscious of my hesitation, he took my hand and brought it to his lips and kissed the palm and fingers. I shivered at the touch of his mouth on my skin. He opened the door to the car and I got in.

That was the first night I spent with Adriaan. He drove me from the party to his house without further discussion, in that moment something between us had been agreed upon. He lived in an apartment occupying the top floors of a substantial townhouse, a place too large for one man. As soon as he unlocked the door and we entered I saw evidence of Gaby: her coat hanging from the rack in the foyer, the gold bracelet lying in the vide poche by the door. The sight of these objects was jarring and I grew flushed, although I also sensed that they remained in the apartment out of negligence rather than any longing on Adriaan's part for her return. He seemed to take no notice of them as he brought me inside and took my coat.

He led me into the living room, then said he would get us something to drink before disappearing into the kitchen. I looked around the large and comfortable room, there was nothing pretentious about the apartment, with its elegant clutter. The bookcases were crammed with volumes but also held little oddments and mementos. Resting on one shelf was a framed photograph of Adriaan with his wife and two children. Kees had not exaggerated, they made a striking family. In fact Gaby was beautiful, more beautiful than I could imagine being, although there was a hint of arrogance in the set of her mouth, the frank gaze she gave to the camera. I continued to examine the image, which must have been taken nearly a decade ago, Kees had said the children were now teenagers, whereas the children in the photograph were no more than four or perhaps five. But Adriaan did not look very different to the man in the photograph, unaged either by time or experience. His hair had gone gray and there were now some lines at his forehead and mouth, but his overall appearance was unchanged.

And I thought that just as Adriaan had remained the same, Gaby too must look as she did in the photograph, her beauty undiminished, as formidable now as she would have been ten years earlier. I was still standing before the photograph when Adriaan returned. He stood behind me and said that the children were now in Portugal with his wife. But perhaps you know this already, he said and then was silent. I turned to face him and then I was no longer thinking of Gaby or the children or the photograph. He pulled me toward him and I reached for him too. In the weeks that followed, some of the items belonging to Adriaan's wife discreetly disappeared, not all at once but piece by piece. The photograph, however, remained.

4.

I looked across the restaurant table at Adriaan. The wine list was open before him, and he tilted it toward me inquiringly. I said that it had been a long day. Let's order a bottle then, he said and signaled for the waiter. Do you know what you want? I nodded, I had only glanced at the menu but we had eaten at the restaurant several times before.

Once the waiter had taken our order Adriaan looked across the table at me again. How is Jana? Adriaan had not yet met Jana—they would meet for the first time that weekend, Jana had asked us to dinner precisely for this purpose. I had hesitated to introduce him to Jana, despite the fact that we had met through her, at least indirectly, at an opening at the Kunstmuseum not long after my arrival in The Hague. Jana had invited me to the event, and after introducing me to a group of people had subsequently been swept away, for obvious reasons she knew a great many more people there than I did.

I remember standing in that cluster of strangers, holding my drink and unable to follow the conversation, which began in English but then slipped into Dutch. At the time, I knew too little still of that language. I noticed Adriaan, because he seemed at ease and because he also said nothing as the conversation accelerated around us. I was silent for so long that I began to wonder if I could slip away, it was strange to remain at the edge of the group saying nothing. At that moment, Adriaan asked if I wanted another drink. I said yes, and then as he took the empty glass from my hand he paused and asked if I wished to join him.

I was relieved to leave that company. We walked through the gallery full of Mondrians and he said that he was very fond of the museum and its collection, it was one of his favorite places in the city. The openings were always strange to him, though, the galleries full of people talking to one another and ignoring the art altogether. Of course, he was doing the same thing right now, he didn't have a leg to stand on. I laughed and then he introduced himself. As we continued walking through the gallery I said that I was new to the city and did not yet know the museum. He said that in that case I was lucky, there were many wonderful things to discover.

The encounter was not very much more than that, but

after we had parted ways he returned and asked for my phone number. I remember that he made the request in a manner that was entirely natural and I also remember the jolt of pleasure I felt as I saw him coming back through the crowd. I gave him my number and later that evening he sent a message. He asked if we could meet again and I sent a single word reply: Yes. Such a response was not in character for me, not in its brevity and not in its unequivocal nature, it was as if I had been influenced by the directness of his own correspondence. That was, I thought, the prospect offered by a new relationship, the opportunity to be someone other than yourself.

When I told Jana about Adriaan she seemed almost perplexed, or perhaps it was some other feeling that crept upon her—in her expression I saw her image of me shift. She had not thought of me as the kind of woman who paired off with a man so quickly. It was only for a brief moment and then she was her usual self, she asked his name and then said she didn't know him but looked forward to meeting him. I thought her voice was overly bright, I told her that I didn't know that it would come to that. But it did come to that, over the course of the following weeks and then months and when Jana had suggested dinner it had been impossible to refuse.

Now, as I looked at Adriaan and he asked how Jana was, I was struck by how little thought or anxiety it seemed to cause him, the idea of meeting her. That again illustrated the differences in our character, such things were never so simple to me. My mind moved in circles, I had been apprehensive about bringing them together, but in his ease I was now reassured. She is fine, I said. I was there last night for dinner. It was odd, something happened in the street, there were police.

Was anybody hurt?

I don't know.

At that moment the waiter arrived with the wine, and then with bottled water and a plate of amuse-bouches. Adriaan waited with his face fixed in a patient grimace, he no longer experienced these small attentions as anything other than a ritual to be endured. When at last the waiter had gone, Adriaan leaned forward and placed his hand on mine, as if to reassert our solitude. The gesture was reassuring rather than erotic, the touch of a friend or even a father, although it could turn on a dime, its intention mutable.

In any case, he said. Please don't move to Jana's neighborhood.

His voice was simultaneously concerned and a little playful, as if the words were a form of flirtation or invitation. I thought of his own home, the furnishings that had been chosen by his wife, the closed doors of the children's bedrooms. The house had once belonged to his parents, and despite the fact that it had been extensively renovated, converted into two apartments because the place was too big for a single family, it remained the house he had spent the long years of his childhood in. That comfort was alien to me, we had moved so frequently when I was young that there was no one place I would think of as my childhood home, we were mostly arriving and then leaving, those years were all motion.

It was not the case with Adriaan, and I thought it was for this reason that he seemed so little troubled by the material remains of his marriage, all those things I would have removed at the moment of my desertion, out of pain and pique—the chair purchased by Gaby, the books on the shelves and the art they had selected together. He did not feel the complexity of those objects and their history, no matter where he was he never looked anything other than a man at home. I smiled and squeezed his hand in return. That tranquility was what had drawn me to him, but at the same time I understood a little better the determination with which Gaby had decorated the place and filled it with her belongings, the degree to which she was trying to occupy a foreign territory, in that action I was able to see beyond the failed marriage, and further into Adriaan's past.

Later that night, after we had returned to his apartment and fallen asleep in what until recently had been his conjugal bed but was now indisputably ours, I awoke. It was the middle of the night and Adriaan was fast asleep, his long limbs bare on the linen beside me. I reached over and touched him but he did not move, his skin smooth and still. After a moment, I rose to my feet and left the bedroom, closing the door gently. The darkness of the hall pooled around me. I fumbled for the light switch and went into the kitchen. I poured a glass of water. Idly, I looked out the window at the street below. It was mostly empty, at the far end I could see the outlines of a man and a woman. They were leaning into each other as they walked, moving a little and then stopping, moving a little and then stopping. At one point, the woman turned her head and glanced around them. I leaned forward, pressing my face to the glass.

The couple linked hands and hurried down the street. Another second and they had disappeared. Their manner had turned furtive, as if they sensed that they were being observed, and I wondered if they had seen me watching from the window. Perhaps they were involved in something illicit, or something that newly appeared so to them— the way we understood our own behavior shifted according to whether or not we thought we were being seen. I moved away from the window and went into the living room. I found myself again staring at the photograph of Gaby and Adriaan and the children—the children, whom I had not yet met, and whom I could not entirely envision. I wondered at the life they'd had here with their parents, how they had filled these rooms, what they missed now they were so far away, in another country altogether. I wondered if they knew their father was seeing another woman, and if so how they might feel: angry, wary, indifferent.

The idea of meeting them was difficult to grasp, I could not imagine how such an encounter might unfold, myself and these now teenaged children. There was a noise in the bedroom and I looked up from the photograph. I heard Adriaan get up from the bed. After a brief silence he called out. I'm here, I said, and I quickly moved away from the bookcase, I couldn't sleep. He appeared in the doorway. My darling, come back to bed. I stared at him, he had never used that particular term of endearment before. His voice was affectionate and familiar and the thought occurred to me at once: he must have said these words to Gaby, that designation must have belonged to her, *My darling, come back to bed.* A shiver of apprehension moved through my body. I stepped closer to him, his eyes were hazy with sleep and for a moment I wasn't certain that he was awake. *It's me,* I almost said, and opened my mouth.

He put his hands on my shoulders, his touch clumsy, and I stiffened. What time is it? he asked. His voice was calm and impersonal, as though he were speaking to a stranger. It's two, I said. He nodded as if digesting this information, his eyes almost closed again into slumber. I

couldn't sleep, I added, I didn't want to wake you. He
yawned and then suddenly leaned forward and kissed me
on the neck and then mouth, his hands on my back and then
slipping down. Come back to bed, he whispered again, his
breath in my ear.

In a minute, I said and pulled away. What are you doing, he asked, his voice still slow and drowsy. Is something
wrong? I shook my head. I just couldn't sleep, I repeated, it's
nothing. I'll be there in a moment. He nodded and kissed
me again, as if we were a couple living together, as if this
were already routine—she suffers from occasional insomnia, whereas I sleep like a log, I could sleep standing in a
train carriage, it must be very irritating for her—perhaps
that had been true of him and Gaby, perhaps he had said
those very words in describing their marriage.

He retreated from the room. I watched him go and,
once I was sure that he had returned to bed—the soft creak
of the springs, the sound of a body shifting on the mattress—
I looked up at the photograph of Gaby on the bookshelf. I
realized that I had the wishful habit of thinking of her in
the past tense, as if she and everything she represented were
firmly contained, although I knew that was untrue, *she is
still with us*. Even this life that was everywhere around me,
the life she'd had within the walls of this apartment, was
not necessarily confined to the past, it could jolt itself into

the present with a mere phone call, a single airplane ticket, a moment of somnambulation.

I returned to the bedroom. Adriaan rolled over and faced me, he wasn't asleep at all. He looked more alert than he had earlier, and when he looked at me I knew this time that he was seeing me and no one else. Is everything okay? he asked tentatively. I got into the bed. Everything is fine, I said, I had some water, I feel much better. And he nodded and pulled me close, his body warm. Good, he said. He already sounded as if sleep were approaching, he had been quickly reassured. Good night, I said, but I didn't know if he heard, he was slipping away again, his arm across my chest and his head heavy upon my shoulder.

5.

The next morning we shared a breakfast of cheese and bread in the apartment, Adriaan made coffee using an expensive machine that generated a great deal of noise and then produced a coffee capped with mountains of milk foam. As he handed me the cup I asked if Gaby was responsible for the machine. Who else? he said and we both laughed.

He didn't say anything about the previous night, and his manner was so perfectly natural that I wondered if it had happened at all. After we ate and dressed he drove me to the nearby bus stop. He kissed me and said that he would text me later. As I got out of the car, I saw the bus at the far end of the street. I leaned over and said goodbye again through the open window. He smiled and kissed me a second time. The bus was fast approaching, but I stood for a moment and watched until his car turned the corner.

It was drizzling again. I ran across the street and joined the other passengers, their faces stoic beneath the shadow of their upraised umbrellas, the scene like a painting. We boarded the bus in an orderly line, in the atomized fashion of commuters. There were no seats available but it didn't matter, the Court was only a few stops from Adriaan's apartment. As I disembarked, I saw that there were a handful of demonstrators gathered outside, supporters of a former West African president currently on trial, in what was one of the higher profile cases at the Court. As I entered the building, one of the demonstrators pressed a flyer into my hands with a small gesture of supplication.

Perhaps because of this polite but insistent demand, I began reading the piece of paper as I crossed the lobby. It was covered in English and French text, the tone of the prose strident: The arrest and trial of the former president was nothing short of illegal, the paper declared, the entire affair completely underhanded. Imagine the emotions of the former president, given no opportunity to contest the legality of the arrest and simply handed from one set of enemies to another! This was the true face of neocolonialism, this apparatus of Western imperialism, this Court. The case against the former president was paper thin, built by the U.S. State Department and the Elysée, a question of policy rather than justice. A coup d'état, executed by men in white gloves, for which the Court was simply the façade—

I stopped reading, folding the piece of paper and slipping it into my bag. The claims were not unfamiliar to me or to anyone who worked at the Court. The record was unfortunately blunt: the Court had primarily investigated and made arrests in African countries, even as crimes against humanity proliferated around the world. It was true that the record did not reflect the complexities of the Court's jurisdiction, nor its limited means of enforcement. It was true that the record did not include the numerous preliminary investigations the Court had made into situations around the world, including Western powers. But a narrative becomes persuasive not through complexity but conviction, and as I entered the elevator and then the offices, I looked at my colleagues and wondered how they felt, the first time they had been handed such a flyer, what their reactions might have been.

The matter was quickly pushed from my mind when, almost as soon as I arrived at my desk, I was told that Bettina wished to speak to me. I hurried across the floor and knocked on the glass door of her office, she glanced up and motioned for me to enter. Bettina's official title was Head of the Language Services Section, she had been the person to interview and then hire me. She oversaw a relatively large number of staff—ten interpreters, in addition to the translators who provided services to various departments of the Court. She was not unkind and might even have been essentially warm in character, it was impossible for me to know. She was not only my direct superior but was also under considerable pressure at all times, the expression on her face was often a grim rictus of apprehension, she was only waiting for things to go wrong.

Now, she asked how I was while continuing to frown at her computer screen. After a brief pause I said that I was well. She nodded and then without further ado said that what she was about to tell me was confidential, at least for the time being. She finally looked up at me, I was still standing in front of her desk. Please, sit down, she said apologetically, I realized as I met her gaze that she was more than usually harried.

She began again. The Court had succeeded in extraditing a well-known jihadist who stood accused of four counts of crimes against humanity and five counts of war crimes. The authorities surrendered him earlier that day, and he was being transported to a plane as we spoke. This is strictly confidential, she said again, even at the Court only a handful of individuals are aware of the arrest, the warrant was issued only a few days ago. I must ask you not to share this with your colleagues. The situation is volatile.

She stopped, as if to gather her thoughts. We expect that the accused will land in The Hague just after midnight, at which point he will be transferred to the Detention Center.

I would like you to be on hand, in order to provide interpretive services. He will need to be read his rights, and of
course there will be other issues, he may have questions or
requests or practical matters to communicate. It's very difficult to predict the mood of the accused once they are
detained, often they are in a state of shock or denial.

We expect the accused will speak French, she continued. That is the official language of his country and we do
not anticipate that there will be any issues of comprehension. She handed me a file. You shouldn't need that tonight,
she said apologetically. But if you have a moment to review
the material that would be good. He will be tired, I hope
you will not need to be there for too long. Of course, you
will be reimbursed any travel expenses, take a taxi if need be.
Her gaze shifted, I could detect a certain excitation in her
manner, I saw that her hands were trembling very slightly.

Again, Bettina said and I looked up from her hands.
Again, this is strictly confidential and is not to be mentioned to your colleagues, or indeed anyone. The Court is
proceeding with caution, as you know it is a pivotal time
for the organization. I nodded. I knew that an arrest meant
that the Court would be full of observers, that the live feeds
would be closely watched, each word spoken heard many
more times than usual. You will need to be there at one in the
morning, Bettina said. She looked down at her papers, and

then said, I wonder what he will be like? She did not seem to require a response to this question, and I turned to go.

Later, I sat at my desk with the file open before me. I felt a little self-conscious, I could hear Bettina's words in my ear, her injunction to secrecy. But my colleagues were absorbed in their own work and I wanted to familiarize myself with the basics of the situation, the key dates and names and locations, though as Bettina herself had said, even this information was likely unnecessary for the purposes of this evening, for what would only be a brief encounter. I began reading. The accused was a member and then leader of an Islamist militant faction that had seized control of the capital only five years earlier. The faction had immediately enforced Sharia law in the occupied territory, banning music, forcing women to wear the burqa, and setting up religious tribunals. He was only the second jihadist to be detained by the Court, and many of the charges were based on the persecution of women—in this case, the forced marriage, repeated rape, and sexual enslavement of girls and women. There were also counts of torture and religious-based persecution, including the desecration of sacred graves.

The file included a small note to the effect that although the case was significant for being only the second to include among the charges persecution based on gender, the fact remained that the nationality of the accused would do little to counter the growing consensus that the Court suffered from a bias against African countries. I thought of the flyer and the demonstrators outside. Affixed to the file was a photograph of the accused. He was on the street, looking to one side as if aware that his image was being captured, his body in motion and his expression furtive. His face was partially concealed by a headscarf, but his eyes were extraordinarily piercing; the remainder of his features were tired and otherwise unremarkable.

I returned to my apartment after work, I thought I might try to sleep in the early part of the evening, I didn't know how long I would be kept at the Detention Center, it might be a matter of minutes or hours. As Bettina had said, it was difficult to predict in what condition the accused would arrive, whether he would be in a state of shock or rage, whether he would be utterly silent or whether questions and accusations and counteraccusations would pour out of him, whether he would simply be tired from his journey, like a businessman disembarking a long-haul flight, or whether he would be in a state of physical collapse. I ate dinner and then rested fitfully, curled up on the bed with the duvet pulled over me. I was unable really to sleep, it was only early evening and the pending assignment weighed on me.

As I lay there, the day outside still carrying traces of light, the sound of the neighbors audible through the walls of my apartment, it was the photograph, the image of this man, that most troubled me. He did not look the way I expected, his face did not live up to the magnitude of the crimes I had read about in the dossier. It was not that he looked either innocent or guilty, it was more that his face was utterly without depth.

In a few hours, I would meet this man, who would then no longer be a name and a photograph, a list of actions and accusations, but a person in the world. I didn't know if I was prepared for that, it seemed almost impossible to fathom—at some point he had crossed a boundary and his personhood had been hollowed out. Maybe the indeterminacy of the photograph was accurate, and was in fact preparing me for the nature of the encounter to come. I checked my phone, there were no messages. I thought of Adriaan, I closed my eyes and tried again to sleep.

I departed for the Detention Center a little before one in the morning. The streets were empty as the taxi pulled up to the curb. When I closed the door behind me and announced my destination, I saw the driver look up, I asked him if he knew where the building was and he nodded.

As we drove through the city in the direction of the

dunes, he continued to watch me in the rearview mirror, as if speculating what function I served, perhaps I did not conform to his notion of how a lawyer, a judge, an official of the Court would appear. Maybe he imagined something entirely more sordid, given the late hour, maybe he thought I was a paid escort servicing one of the men detained in the center, it was not impossible. I looked down at what I was wearing, I was dressed conservatively enough, in what is usually described as "business casual"—but I had been told that this was exactly how escorts dressed, the ones that were not walking the street, the ones who were under considerable pressure to be discreet, who had famous and powerful clients, the kind of men who might conceivably be held in the Detention Center. I shifted my weight in the back of the taxi, pulling the hem of my skirt lower, I worried that I had dressed in a manner that was unintentionally provocative, the man had made me thoroughly self-conscious.

I was therefore relieved to arrive at the Detention Center, which sat on the edge of the city, not too far from the Court. In the dark of night it looked forbidding, there were high walls and CCTV cameras, it was a prison in all but name. I paid the taxi driver, who asked if I didn't want him to wait, I blushed and said that I did not know how long I would be, and that I would call a taxi when I wanted to leave. He handed me his business card and said that he would be working all night, the gesture felt salacious and also a little sad, and I dropped the card into my pocket, feeling as if I needed to wash my hands. The car lingered as I pressed the buzzer, luckily the door opened at once. I passed through a medieval gatehouse and then through security, my bag was taken away and my passport examined.

I was handed a badge and told to wait, the guard indicated a row of plastic chairs. I clipped the badge to my jacket and sat down. The area—less a reception or lobby and more a corridor along which some chairs had been arranged—was clean and anonymous, I could have been waiting in any municipal building, at an American DMV, for example. This feeling only grew as the hour passed two in the morning, and then approached three, the sensation of waiting for a slow and truculent bureaucracy increasing, I had never been in this situation and yet, as my eyes grew bleary with fatigue, I felt exactly as if I had been here before, everything about the act of waiting had removed the specificity of the circumstances, I could no longer remember for whom I was waiting, only that I was waiting for someone who might never arrive, and that I might never leave this vestibule.

A little after three, the door behind me abruptly opened. I stood, a uniformed guard indicated that I should follow. My mouth was suddenly dry, we made our way down a series of harshly lit corridors and points of entry, the guard swiping cards and entering codes until we reached what appeared to be a cellblock. The doors were shut save one, through which I could see a number of Court officials. They were speaking in not especially quiet tones, their voices reverberating down the corridor, and I found myself worrying about the occupants in the other cells, whose sleep was surely being disrupted. As we reached the open cell, the officials greeted me courteously, with a brusque air of professional urgency. After I greeted them there was a pause during which no one said anything.

Finally, one of the officials cleared his throat. There had been some difficulty in persuading the accused to leave the plane, for a time he refused to get up from his seat. He had now arrived, the official added, he was on his way. I nodded, I wondered how the accused had issued his refusal, if it was in the manner of a toddler refusing to get out of a stroller, or if it was in the manner of a political protester refusing to abandon a site, or perhaps his legs had simply given out on him and he had found himself unable to stand. The space we had gathered in was somewhere between a cell and a dormitory room, with a single bed and a desk, and a toilet in one corner. Affixed to the wall was a flat-screen television. There was a large window at the far side of the room, lined with bars.

We heard the sound of the cellblock door opening in the distance and we turned at once. Despite the fatigue and the provisional nature of the setting, a ripple of expectation moved through the room. The door slammed shut and then we heard the sound of feet shuffling down the corridor and past the other cells, with what seemed incredible slowness. I was sure that the other detainees were awake and listening, perhaps remembering their own arrival at the Detention Center, the start of what was an indeterminate and therefore all the more painful state of waiting. The sound of footfalls grew louder, and then came to a halt and the accused appeared in the doorway of the cell.

He was accompanied by two guards, he was wearing traditional robes and looked so much older than in the photograph, which could not have been taken very long ago, that I felt an immediate and inexplicable tightening in my throat. He glared at each of us in turn, he stood with his mouth pursed, it was clear that he was disgusted with the situation. We stood in an uneasy cluster until one of the Court officials stepped forward, his expression awkward and even embarrassed. He hesitated and then looked at me and I moved closer to the accused. After another pause, the official at last began, his voice apologetic and uncertain. I am going to read you your rights.

I began interpreting immediately, angling my body toward the accused and speaking in a low voice into his ear. The man jerked his head away, as if irritated by a mosquito or some other airborne insect, he gave no sign whatsoever of listening. The official paused, I finished speaking a few moments later and then the official asked if he had any questions. I interpreted, the accused exhaled noisily and I trailed off, the words withering in the air. The accused began speaking rapidly in Arabic and as he continued, now looking angrily at the official and gesturing at the room around him—which was, I gathered from his tone and manner, evidently substandard or objectionable in some way—panic surged up inside me. I looked at the official, who was staring at me expectantly. I shook my head—I knew hardly any Arabic—and turned back to the accused.

Finally, the accused stared at me and asked—in French, which he spoke haltingly but I thought fluently—why he had not been provided with an Arabic language interpreter. I began to apologize, he interrupted—holding up one hand and now refusing to look at me, as if the mere sight of me were offensive, perhaps because I was the sole woman in the room or perhaps it was the sound of my French that was so problematic—and began speaking again in Arabic, his voice louder, almost bellicose. I could see that the Court officials were rattled and beginning to hold me responsible for the situation, it was obvious that I was failing at my assigned task, if through no clear fault of my own. The man needed to be read his rights in a language that he could understand, and which I did not appear to speak, and yet—because I did not know what else to do, and because the situation seemed to require that I do something—I began to recite the text again in my offending French, speaking over him and then asking at last if he had understood.

Do you understand? I repeated.

Yes, he said at last, in French.

Abruptly, he moved to the bed and sat down. I saw that he was exhausted. He lay down and closed his eyes and then in seconds—so quickly that it was almost beyond belief—was snoring as he slept on the bed. We watched him for a moment, and then one of the officials tilted his head toward the door and quietly we filed out of the room and the guard closed it behind us. The official looked at me and said, We will request someone who speaks Arabic. I nodded. I almost felt sorry for him, he said, shaking his head. I did not agree, I could not help but feel that we had been manipulated in some way—although to what end I could not say, the accused had achieved nothing by this little drama, and he of course had the right to an interpreter working in the language of his choice.

The official told me I could go, it was now—he looked at his watch—nearly four in the morning. I pulled on my coat and followed one of the uniformed guards down the maze of corridors and back through security. The guard called a taxi, which arrived very soon after. I sat in the car as we drove through the city, it was still completely dark outside, without a hint of dawn, the night appeared unceasing. We reached my apartment, I paid the driver, who waited until I had entered the building. Now at last there was a barely perceptible lightening of the sky, the sun would be up in a couple hours. I checked my messages, Adriaan had sent me a text some time ago, asking how I was, and then another asking what he might bring to Jana's, if he could bring something more than a bottle of wine. I lay down without responding and fell asleep.

6.

I received another text from Adriaan later that morning. He thought he might bring food from the Indonesian
restaurant around the corner from his apartment, to save
Jana the trouble of cooking. I read the message and then
curled back into bed. The arrival of these texts, their ordinary nature, had given me a sense of reassurance that I did
not know I had needed. The tumult of the previous night
had affected me more than I had understood.

This sensation was with me still when I later woke
at noon. It was a Saturday, the Court would likely make
the announcement on Monday, I would not be able to speak
of last night's events for at least a little longer. As I lay in
bed, I wondered if the accused had woken from his sudden
slumber—if slumber it was, and not merely the pretense of
it—startled to find himself in such a strange and hostile

place, having been in dreams transported elsewhere. If he'd had the overwhelming sensation that he was the wrong person in the wrong place. I realized that I'd felt some minor version of that myself, as I stood in the cell, unable to comprehend his words, unable to perform the task that had been assigned to me, as if caught in a case of mistaken identity.

I picked up my phone and responded to Adriaan's text. I said that I thought that bringing food would be kind and much appreciated, I would let Jana know. He responded at once and said that he would see me there. I told him to call if he had any difficulty finding Jana's apartment. But as it turned out, had Adriaan become lost on his way to dinner, had he stumbled down the wrong path or into harm's way, had he called to ask if this was the correct route or if he had taken a wrong turn, I would not have been able to help him, I would not have even answered the phone. I had fallen asleep, in the manner of a narcoleptic—on the sofa, a book on my lap, my head flung back, my phone in the next room so that I could not have heard its ring. Had Adriaan called. But when I awoke, several minutes past eight in the evening, there were no missed calls or messages on my phone and it was already dark outside. I had been asleep for much of the afternoon.

I dressed hurriedly and sent messages to both Adriaan and Jana to say that I was running late. It was now dark, the streets full with the expectation of a night out. I took a taxi, I was already half an hour late and Adriaan would of course be on time. As the driver pulled into the full flow of traffic—it was unusually dense or seemed that way, perhaps because of my impatience, I was aware that Jana and Adriaan had been thrust together in circumstances more uncomfortable and intimate than intended—I leaned forward and peered out the window, it would take at least twenty minutes to reach Jana's at this rate.

The traffic did not improve, by the time I arrived at Jana's apartment it was nearly nine o'clock, and Adriaan had been there for an hour. You're late, Jana said as she opened the door. Her tone was far from reproachful and she was smiling, she looked unusually relaxed. I was nonplussed by her appearance, she looked very different, so that I almost did not recognize her. She lingered before the door longer than was normal, as if to prevent me from entering, for a moment I thought there was something she needed to tell me. Behind her, I could see Adriaan standing in the kitchen, a glass of wine in hand. He was watching us with a curious expression, I wondered what Jana had been saying to him.

She finally said, Come in, and stepped back almost reluctantly. I looked at Adriaan again as I took off my coat and set down my bag, my expression quizzical, but he either didn't notice or chose to ignore it, he came forward with his glass of wine and kissed me, his manner very natural. I was aware that Jana was watching, at the last moment I angled my cheek toward him and my mouth away, so that his kiss landed awkwardly. I felt my skin grow flushed. I'm sorry I'm late. He shrugged and said that it didn't matter, he seemed amused, he was hovering over me in a way that felt oddly protective, and I wished again that I hadn't been so delayed.

How have you two been getting along, I asked. They looked at each other and smiled, I was looking not at Adriaan but at Jana. She had put on lipstick and eye makeup, which she did not usually bother to do, and it might have been simply that I was not used to seeing her lips and eyes colored and delineated in this way, her features so emphatic. I realized, belatedly, that she had likely applied the makeup for Adriaan's sake; certainly she had not done so for mine. I wondered then what it was like to be a man, so often surrounded by such deliberate features, more vivid than actual nature.

I looked at Jana, and then again at Adriaan. I saw that some intimacy had been established between them. It wasn't surprising, in fact it was something that I should have predicted from the outset, they were both personable and even seductive people. I thought this must be the reason for Jana's inexplicable transformation, in the end it couldn't be put down to lipstick and mascara, that was only the physical

manifestation of a more intangible shift. It suddenly occurred to me that they made sense as a couple, I thought
that Gaby was probably a woman like Jana, confident and
forthright, someone who was a mirror to Adriaan. Couples
were often this way, even when the resemblance wasn't
there to begin with. Warily, I watched as Jana and Adriaan
continued to look at each other, now much longer than
seemed necessary. Jana was grinning foolishly, or so it appeared to me.

I felt a surge of jealousy. We did okay, Adriaan said, and
his voice was casual. He turned to look at me, his gaze was
warm and he was smiling, he did not seem as if he had anything to hide. She put me through the wringer but I'm fine,
I survived. Although this sentence was spoken to me, and
although Adriaan continued looking at me with his friendly
and transparent gaze, I nonetheless experienced his words
as further evidence of complicity between Jana and Adriaan.
Jana was still looking at him and now she laughed too
loudly, tossing her hair extravagantly, a gesture I was not
familiar with, it was if she had remade herself entirely for
the occasion.

I did not! she exclaimed flirtatiously. I did nothing of
the sort. I only asked some questions, I'm very protective of
my friend, you know she's quite alone here—words that
somehow made me feel as if I did not belong in this city or

country or even in this room. She wrapped her arm around my shoulder, a gesture that was surely affectionate, but which came across as bizarre and out of character, she was not usually physically demonstrative. She squeezed my shoulder, an embrace that recollected my encounter with Kees at the party, when I had first learned that Adriaan was married. I must have looked uneasy, or perhaps he had himself observed the similarity between the two embraces, because Adriaan now frowned a little and after a moment Jana lowered her arm. I cleared my throat, I asked if we shouldn't eat. Jana turned away abruptly, she said, Adriaan brought Indonesian takeaway, from a place I don't know.

She had set the table, there were cloth napkins and place mats and candles. Let's eat, Jana said. The food is in the oven, keeping warm. We didn't know how late you would be. I realized that neither of them had asked for an explanation for my tardy arrival. She began taking foil containers of food out of the oven, she shook her head when I offered to help, and told us to sit down.

Adriaan and I stood by the dining table in silence, staring at the flickering candles—Jana or Adriaan or someone had taken the trouble to light them. How is work, how have you been? Jana called out. She was making a great deal of noise as she retrieved the food from the oven, banging the door open and shut and clattering plates. It's fine, I shouted back, a reply that seemed barely to register. A part of me was relieved, it would have been difficult to talk about work without mentioning the arrest, I would have been speaking around something that loomed so large in my thoughts that they would have sensed it through its omission.

There was more noise from the kitchen, and after glancing at Adriaan, I went to Jana, saying, Let me help you, and together we began ferrying out dishes of food to the table. The food looked delicious and Jana was quick to compliment Adriaan on his choices, I never could have ordered so well, she said. It was a strange and slightly inane compliment and one that was almost certainly a lie, Jana loved to cook and eat out and at any rate it wasn't a particularly stellar achievement, ordering a takeout meal. Jana lifted her glass of wine and said, Well, here we all are. She was still smiling and her voice was vibrating with tension. Adriaan nodded as he raised his glass, he thanked Jana for inviting him into her home, of the three of us he was the only one who seemed truly at ease.

For a moment, Jana and I both watched him serving the food. We were converted into women admiring a man's competence, an absurd and appalling situation. He was only dishing out noodles and rice and chunks of meat onto our plates, and yet I also found myself watching him appreciatively, perhaps because of my awareness of Jana's own admiration. I knew very well that the reason for Jana's present excitement was her own attraction to Adriaan, she could be competitive and would have felt the need to establish primacy in this situation, one that she had initiated, after all, by suggesting dinner in the first place.

As for Adriaan, he might have been thinking or feeling anything. I couldn't tell what he made of Jana, or indeed the entire situation. Perhaps he thought it had been a mistake to agree to the dinner, it was only the three of us, it was obvious that it had been organized so that Jana might get a look at him, so to speak. Meanwhile, Jana was being careful to avoid the subject of Adriaan's marriage and separation, she asked Adriaan a little about his work, the area he lived in, innocuous questions to which she already knew the answers, she did not venture near territory that might be potentially compromising.

The entire exercise had an air of futility and falseness. Adriaan must have been perfectly aware of the fact that Jana knew everything not only about his job and where he lived, but also about his marriage to Gaby and its unresolved state. Nor could the skillful façade of her conversation conceal the fact that Jana also knew that Adriaan knew that she knew, disavowed knowledge reverberated through the room. And yet our behavior did not seem especially strange, people behave with such conscious and unconscious dishonesty all the time. Or perhaps the dishonesty was more concrete, I suddenly thought, perhaps it lay in something they were keeping from me, some argument or agreement between them, and then I wondered if they'd had it out the moment Adriaan arrived, perhaps Jana had let him in and then said, Listen, I want to know how it is between you, I want to know exactly what your intentions are.

She was more than capable of doing such a thing—like Adriaan she could be unusually direct in her manner. Now Jana turned to Adriaan and said playfully, I know you don't approve of a young woman living in this area—I looked up, startled, I had not told Jana this, and yet she was not incorrect in her assessment of him, and how he would feel about the neighborhood, she had intuited a conservatism I doubted he himself would recognize. And it's true, Jana continued, it's not as safe as other parts of the city, just the other day there was an incident. A man was mugged, right outside my front door.

Adriaan lowered his fork to his plate, as if to give Jana his full attention.

The other night, when I was here? I asked and she nodded.

The man is in the hospital. Jana paused. It could have been one of us, it could have been you, she said, looking directly at Adriaan. In fact he was not unlike you, I looked him up, he was wealthy, a professional, probably he was in the area seeing friends for dinner, almost exactly as you are doing now.

But how do you know? I asked. They released the name,

she said. It was in one article, there wasn't that much information, but once I had the name, you know the internet, everything is available. He's a book dealer, a man called Anton de Rijk, he has a business in the Old Town that is very successful. He probably lives in your part of the city, she said to Adriaan. Although the subject matter had suddenly become very serious, her flirtation persisted, taking the form of blunt aggression, it wasn't exactly friendly to hypothesize that it might just as easily have been Adriaan lying in a hospital bed.

Yes, she continued, he was probably visiting friends, on his way to a dinner party, only he never arrived, how long do you think his friends waited before they sat down to eat? An hour? An hour and a half? She stopped, as if remembering that they had only recently been waiting for me to arrive, that they might sit down to dinner. One day you are living an ordinary life with its ordinary ups and downs, and then that life is ripped apart and you can never feel entirely secure again. You spend your days looking over your shoulder, your understanding of the world is changed, you see it as a brittle place, full of hostility.

She picked up her fork and began eating, she had barely touched her food and was obviously hungry. Adriaan said that this was how violence functioned and why it was so effective at disrupting society, that was why terrorism worked. Jana swallowed, setting down her fork and reaching for her glass of wine. Of course, she said abruptly.

Still, something must have gone wrong, Adriaan said. There's no reason to beat a man if all you're after is money, if a man threatens you with violence, if a man asks for your wallet and phone, you give it to him, we all know that.

Yes, but things do go wrong, Jana said. Even the most hardened criminal can panic and go further than he intended, the body is both more resilient and more fragile than one expects, even those who are accustomed to violence can be taken by surprise. Or perhaps the criminal was an amateur, and underestimated his own strength. Or perhaps he acted out of malice, that's also not impossible, is it? Jana shrugged. In a way the intention doesn't matter because whether his attacker—or I suppose attackers, there may have been more than one—acted out of malice or out of panic, the result is the same, the poor man is still in the hospital and you know it's been several days, I can only think that he must have been very badly injured.

Did they catch whoever did it? I asked.

I'm sure they have it under control, she said, they probably already have a suspect, there are CCTV cameras on that block, nothing goes undetected anymore. I always hated the cameras, I thought it was the sign of a surveillance state. But now I find they make me feel a little bit safer, I suppose this is how people become conservative. She sounded a little calmer than before. Being a property owner changes your perception of things whether you like it or not. Even the smallest apartment is enough to do the job, it's difficult not to be contaminated by it, there's a difference between living in theory and living in practice.

She spoke as if home ownership had transformed her completely, as if she'd been buried in the battlements of her apartment, her life ossified. But I knew this wasn't true, that Jana's own situation remained contingent, the stability around us was simply a matter of appearances. That must have been, I realized, what Adriaan had felt when he had returned home to find an empty apartment. I gazed at him across the table, that must have been what he felt when he gathered the children and sat them down, when he searched for the words to tell them that their mother was gone. Every certainty can give way without notice. No one and nothing was exempt from this rule, not even Adriaan.

7.

For a long time, Jana was quiet. Her face was creased with fatigue and worry and I had a vision of her restless in the night, peering out the window, getting out of bed to check that the door was locked. There was no ghost of coquetry in her manner now, nothing that was in the least bit performed, she seemed to have turned completely inward.

Perhaps a full minute later, she looked up and smiled. What a depressing turn to the conversation, that's my fault. She reached for the bottle of wine and poured herself another glass, and then filled both my glass and Adriaan's. I shook my head and said, It's only natural to worry, or words to that effect, words without any particular meaning. The subject had seemed so innocuous, mere small talk—and yet it had cordoned each of us into a private realm, it was as if we had mutually agreed there was nothing more to be said between us.

Let's talk about something else, shall we? Jana smiled at Adriaan and me, as if to reassure us that matters were exactly the same as before. Not too long after that, Adriaan looked at his phone and said that we should be going, and that he would order a car. I asked him mechanically if he hadn't driven, and he shook his head. A little later, his phone pinged. The car had arrived and we stood up. Jana followed us to the door, then reminded us that she had an exhibition opening in several weeks, she hoped we would both come. I nodded and she embraced me quickly before saying she would look forward to seeing us then.

As we sat in the back of the taxi, Adriaan took my hand and then said, I'm going to be away for a week, possibly longer.

For work? I asked. My voice was flat, I was tired from the previous night and the dinner had been wearing. I was disappointed by Adriaan's announcement but my mind was elsewhere, preoccupied with these stories of violence, in the Court and in the street. They changed the register of the city I saw through the windows of the car, I thought of Anton de Rijk and how recently he had walked these very roads. Adriaan was silent for a moment and then he cleared his throat and said, No, I am going to Lisbon to see Gaby and the children. He held my hand a moment longer and then said quietly, I'm going to ask her for a divorce.

I turned now to face him. In the dark, his features appeared tentative, and then soft with misery. I was caught off guard, the distance between my elation—because that was what I had felt upon hearing his words, elation unbidden and uncontrolled, that pulsed through the whole of my body—and his frank unhappiness was overwhelming. I wondered if he had reached this decision reluctantly, a step taken after months of unmet hope and hesitation, an internal debate he had kept from me. He seemed aware of my uncertainty and smiled. I'm not looking forward to it, he said, but there are some things we need to discuss, things that cannot be talked about on the phone or written in an email, and that need to be done face-to-face.

I nodded, I only asked him when he was leaving. Tomorrow, he said. I decided to make the trip a few days ago. My flight is early, I'll need to leave the apartment at five in the morning. Have you booked a car? I asked. He ignored the question and took my hand again. I thought you might like to stay in the apartment while I'm away, he said. You'll have less of a commute in the mornings and it would make me happy to imagine you there. He paused. I don't like to leave you. We haven't known each other for very long, but I want to know that you'll be here when I return.

I'll be here, I said. He took my hands and kissed me. At the time it didn't occur to me to wonder why he needed this assurance, or why a departure of a week required such declarations of intent. Good, he whispered, and I saw that he was relieved, some matter now settled in his mind. We rode in silence back to the house and when we entered the apartment he asked once more, So you will stay? I nodded. He again looked relieved. He said that he would leave keys out for me. It will only be a week, or possibly a little longer, he said and I thought that he was trying to reassure us both.

He was true to his word on this point, departing early the next morning. I awoke some hours later in the oversized bed. It was the first time I had been alone in the apartment. I got up and went out into the hallway. Behind the doors lining the hallway there was only silence. I briefly wondered if Adriaan might have changed his mind, if there would be no key after all, the offer retracted either by intention or by oversight. But he had not forgotten, and when I entered the kitchen I immediately saw a set of keys, resting on the kitchen counter alongside a note that read *I will imagine you here while I'm away.*

I stood in the kitchen and read the note twice. I picked up the keys, I felt a shiver of pleasure. I decided to make a coffee using the ludicrous machine, I looked in the cupboards and found a cup, poured out milk and added water. The machine began to grind and whir, and then to spurt out coffee and milk. I sat at the counter and drank the coffee, I realized how removed the apartment was from the stream of life outside, through the miracles of double glazing and insulation. Alone, the quiet had a different meaning, forlorn and almost burdensome. Suddenly restless, I put my coffee cup down. I had a set of keys, I could come and go as I wished, I had been told to treat the place as my own.

I dressed and made my way down to the street, the area was well serviced by public transportation and within moments I was on a tram running in the direction of the Old Town. I had been on the tram many times of course, but somehow this journey felt subtly different, the city frequently changed before my eyes but now I felt an attachment I had sought but not previously felt, it was as if an anchor had been dropped. I stepped off not too far from the Mauritshuis and stood for a moment in the crush of pedestrians and tourists. I walked down a street at random, and realized it had been some time since I had moved through the city in this way, with this leisure and freedom.

I had been walking for some time when I passed a bookshop with leather-bound volumes in the window. I suddenly remembered Jana's words, *He's a book dealer, a man called*

Anton de Rijk, he has a business in the Old Town that is very success-ful. Giving in to sudden impulse, I circled back and entered, there were not so many bookshops in the Old Town and there was at least some likelihood that this was the one. A young woman looked up as soon as I entered and smiled in a vague but not unfriendly way, I nodded and pretended to examine the shelves. Despite the deliberation with which I perused the titles and the emptiness of the shop—I began to worry that it was not so successful as Jana had thought—the young woman did not approach or speak to me.

Eventually, I went to the desk, my eyes still on the shelves, and she asked if she could help me. I shook my head, I said that I was only browsing and asked if she was the owner of the shop. She laughed, a loud and indecorous sound. Far from it, she said and smiled. I asked how long she had worked at the shop. Three years, she said. It wasn't a bad job, it was quite interesting and the customers were colorful—antiquarian books drew a certain kind of clien-tele, although it wasn't only antiquarian volumes, they sold all kinds of things. Then, because she was silent and I wished to prolong the conversation, I said that I was looking for a history of the city, something that would make a nice gift.

She rose and retrieved several volumes, opening them to display beautiful maps and foldout plates, as I examined the books she said they ranged in price from a hundred euros to considerably more. I asked her when the volumes had been published and she said they were mostly nineteenth century. I touched the morocco binding, they were beautiful things, and although it was more money than I had to spend, I told the woman I would buy one of the books, I thought I might give it to Adriaan.

As she was ringing up the purchase, I asked her who the owner was. She seemed surprised by the question and I said I only asked because the bookshop had a great deal of personality. The statement was inane and yet it was not untrue, you could feel the imprint of the person behind the shop. She said the owner was a man called Anton de Rijk. Quickly, I asked if he was often at the shop and she said that normally he was, but he had unfortunately been called away, when exactly he would be back she couldn't say. I thought she seemed uneasy and yet I couldn't help but ask, Nothing serious, I hope? And after a pause, she shook her head, not in the least, I had only to return in a week or two and I would find him there. A week or two, she repeated, or possibly three. Abruptly she held out the packaged book. I took it from her and thanked her for her help.

I left the shop, the package in my hands. I hardly knew why I had ventured in, or why I had asked so many questions about De Rijk. *A week or two*, she had said, *or possibly three*. I had been obscurely relieved to hear this. When I returned to the apartment I unwrapped the book and held it in my hands, it was strange to see it here, in this room. I placed it on the coffee table and then picked it up and moved it to one of the bookshelves in the living room. I saw that after all it wasn't entirely right, it stood out and looked like a foreign object, with its ornate binding and rubbed edges. In the end I didn't know who it was for. I sat down on the sofa. I missed Adriaan, and for a brief moment I felt stranded in the enormous apartment, as if I had been left behind.

I slept poorly and when I woke the following morning, it was no longer the weekend and it was later than usual. There was no question of returning to my apartment to change, I showered and then put on the same clothes, for the third day now. On a whim, I opened the door to one of the wardrobes in the bedroom, inside was a vast array of pressed shirts and suits, more than one man could reasonably wear. They were a revelation to me in their excess, so many shirts and so carefully arranged. I knew that a cleaner regularly attended to the house, not a cleaner but a housekeeper, who did the shopping and restocked the cupboards when they were bare, who no doubt fetched the dry cleaning and placed the shirts in the wardrobe after removing their plastic covers. I had run into this woman once, outside the apartment, and from the way she had both ignored and scrutinized me, I knew that she was someone who had been in the family's employ long before Gaby's departure.

I left the apartment without tidying up—what days did the housekeeper come to the apartment? Adriaan did not say in his note—locked the door behind me, and carefully placed the keys inside my bag. I boarded the bus around the corner, which quickly reached the shore, and then proceeded parallel to the rolling dunes, in the direction of the Court. Perhaps ten minutes later the bus passed the Detention Center where I had been three nights earlier. In all the months that I had worked at the Court I had only been aware of the Detention Center in principle, I had never imagined it within the context or geography of the city. It had remained as abstract as the photographs displayed on the information boards in the lobby of the Court, photographs that failed to communicate the brutal reality of the place I had seen only the other night—a dark enclosure, standing in utter contrast to the light-filled transparency of the Court itself, a building defined by its density.

By daylight, the Detention Center was less sinister than it had appeared by night, and there was something almost matter-of-fact about its presence on the side of the road. The bus did not stop outside the Detention Center and I saw the wall and outline of the building only fleetingly through the window, it was simply another one of those buildings that exist in the landscape in which you live, of which you never take real notice and whose purpose you never know. There are prisons and far worse all around us, in New York there was a black site above a bustling food court, the windows darkened and the rooms soundproofed so that the screaming never reached the people sitting below. People eating their sandwiches and sipping their cappuccinos, who had no idea of what was taking place directly above them, no idea of the world in which they were living.

But none of us are able to really see the world we are living in—this world, occupying as it does the contradiction between its banality (the squat wall of the Detention Center, the bus running along its ordinary route) and its extremity (the cell and the man inside the cell), is something that we see only briefly and then do not see again for a long time, if ever. It is surprisingly easy to forget what you have witnessed, the horrifying image or the voice speaking the unspeakable, in order to exist in the world we must and we do forget, we live in a state of I know but I do not know.

This is why I was able to see the Detention Center again by daylight and then, moments later, disembark the bus and enter the Court, greeting the security guards as I always did, exactly as if nothing had changed. It was easy to slip into the crowd of bodies moving through the security checkpoints, swiping their badges and passing through the metal detectors, easy to walk across the courtyard and into the building itself.

But then, as I reached the entrance to the building, I saw Amina standing by the door, she gestured to me and almost before I had reached her, as if she had only been waiting until I was within earshot, she said, They're moving you to Chamber I. I looked at her in surprise. You're going to be my replacement, when I go on leave. She took my arm, giving it a gentle squeeze. This is good, isn't it? I asked her. She nodded, Yes, it's a very good sign, and I squeezed her hand in return. Come, she said. And together we entered the building.

8.

Inside the elevator, Amina leaned against the wall and recovered her breath. She was now easily winded, the baby inside pushing hard against her lungs. She looked at me and then said her mother was due to arrive from Senegal soon, she would be going on leave in a few weeks. As we exited the elevator and made our way to the booth, she asked me if I was familiar with the case and I nodded, the details were well-known throughout the Court. The trial had been running for several months and was of great significance, it was the first time a former head of state had been brought to trial at the Court and proceedings had caused considerable furor in the international press.

And then of course there was the matter of the protesters who had for months been gathering at the Court on behalf of the accused, handing out those flyers and holding up signs. As we sat down, Amina told me that I'd be working in the booth with her for the week, in order to familiarize myself with the situation. She handed me a file. There shouldn't be any issue of comprehension, she said, the language thus far has been perfectly straightforward. She nodded to the file, which now sat on the desk before me, and I opened it. According to the case summary, circumstances had developed very rapidly, during a relatively narrow time frame of four to five months, in the wake of a disputed election. The national electoral commission and outside observers called the election in favor of the accused's opposition. The accused refused to cede power, despite the fact that there was also a constitutional limit of ten years for any presidency, a term the accused had already served. He then indulged in some creative accounting, nullifying the votes in districts where his opponent polled strongly, ordered the army to close the borders, and barred all foreign media.

The accused then—I began to scan the file more hurriedly, one eye on the officials who were filing into the courtroom below, the session would begin soon—formed an army of mercenaries and began a process of ethnic cleansing, leading to death squads and mass graves. The UN sent peacekeeping troops, the African Union demanded that the accused step down from power, he was entirely unrepentant. His opponent retaliated, civil war ensued. Eventually, in the wake of French and United Nations air strikes, the opposition forces and the UN captured the accused and placed him under house arrest. This was approximately five months after the disputed election. If peacekeeping troops had not been present, it was assumed that the accused would have been executed, but the UN argued with some force that he should be tried in an international court, and now here he was, and had been for some years awaiting trial.

I closed the dossier and placed it to one side. Beneath it was a large photograph of the former president. He was looking into the distance, one arm raised and his mouth open as if he were delivering oratory. There were people visible behind him, their shapes blurred so that they were accumulations of color rather than distinct figures, he might have been speaking at a rally in the final days before the disputed election. He was wearing an expensive suit and tie and even in the photograph his body was rigid with energy and tension. In the background, I could make out large placards and banners.

Amina gestured to the public gallery, which was also in the mezzanine, adjacent to the interpreters' booths. Inside, there were numerous attendees. The former president's supporters, Amina said. In the second row I saw the man who had given me the flyer outside the Court. He was talking with several other supporters, his face as vulnerable as before, it was a pulpy mess of emotion and I remembered the former president's message to these supporters, as he

boarded the plane bound for The Hague. *Don't cry, be strong*—
a slogan that was subsequently emblazoned across newspa-
per headlines, that perhaps even now was being whispered
by his supporters in the public gallery.

There's some press today, she continued, new counsel
for the defense will appear and the addition is apparently of
some significance. She nodded to the group occupying one
section of the public gallery. This trial is quite a spectacle,
she whispered, more than usual, I would say. From the van-
tage point of the booth we could observe the courtroom
below, the prosecution to one side and the defense to the
other, the judges at the front and the witness stand at the
back. Nearly every person on the floor seemed to be en-
gaged in urgent activity, clustered around computer moni-
tors, or flipping through large binders. I glanced at Amina
but her attention was now fixed on her notes, she had told
me in the elevator that she would do the bulk of the interpreting today, to give me a chance to acclimate.

I looked back down, there was some movement on the
floor and I saw that the counsel for the defense had arrived,
claiming the left side of the courtroom. They were dressed
in robes, their manner somewhat circumspect as they nodded to their junior associates. I observed the three men,
something in the sight of them was troubling, I watched as
they set their papers down, conversed with the assistants
who fluttered around them. It was only after some contem-

plation that I realized, with horror, that one of the three men was Kees, the man from the party, Gaby's friend.

I quickly leaned back in my chair, afraid that he might see me in the booth, although such a thing was unlikely. For a moment, I wondered if I was mistaken; although I remembered Adriaan saying that he was a defense lawyer, *one of the best in the country*, his appearance seemed too implausible. I looked back down, at the man's lustrous head of hair, no less coiffed here in the courtroom than it had been at the party. On the one hand it was impossible to reconcile the man in robes with the man I had met that night, on the other hand it was undoubtedly the same person, it was not the person but the context that made his presence so incomprehensible. He himself remained exactly the same, as I watched he made the same ridiculous movements, the hand to the hair, those assorted and imperious gestures.

However, in this context they mysteriously acquired gravitas, the junior associates and also the other lawyers nodded in response to the flamboyant flapping of his hands without a trace of irony or derision. When Adriaan had told me he was a defense lawyer I had imagined that he defended white-collar criminals, perpetrators of tax fraud or corporate malfeasance, simply because he seemed so petty a man. Of course, I'd known it was equally possible he represented people accused of manslaughter or robbery, the person who had assaulted Anton de Rijk, for example—crimes of a more serious nature, crimes that, even as they remained individual, could not be described as trivial.

But that he should be a defense lawyer for crimes of this scale, crimes of historical significance, that he should appear here in this courtroom—this was entirely too incongruous, he did not seem as if he would have the gravity of mind to discuss such matters, much less the concentration to make the necessary arguments. It was not that I thought a man could not be superficial and cunning and also a brilliant lawyer or politician—there were many men and women of considerable social repute who were nothing less than reprehensible in their private lives—it was more that I couldn't believe the men and women in the Court would take him seriously, it seemed extraordinary that they would trust this man, a man of the flimsiest construction, in this most critical of matters.

And yet, as I observed the scene below, I saw that he was in a position of no small authority within the team, as he gave his directives they listened with care and even enthusiasm, they seemed to hang on his words, it was obvious that he was not simply respected but admired and even feared. Across the room, the prosecution was observing him warily, I could imagine that he had a reputation for ruthlessness and deviousness, and I wondered if that was another reason why Adriaan had greeted him with such suspicion, because of his professional capacity for deception.

I thought it odd that Adriaan had not mentioned that Kees was likely or even qualified to appear at the Court, and it occurred to me that Adriaan knew very little of the work that I did, and that he had not fully imagined the parts of my life in which he did not share. In fact Kees would have a far greater understanding of my daily life; if at that party I had happened to say that I worked at the Court, it was possible that we would have had an entirely different conversation, that he would have then seemed to me an intelligent and informed man, who knew a great deal about a world I was only just entering. I might then have been more open to his advances, I might have taken his number or even gone home with him that night, rather than Adriaan.

The thought was disquieting—that our identities should be so mutable, and therefore the course of our lives. As I stared down at him through the glass, that alternative version of events seemed to manifest, filling the air between us. Suddenly, Kees straightened up and turned toward the side door of the courtroom, his face broadening into the same wolfish grin I remembered so well from the party. He spread his arms in greeting, I craned my neck and I saw that the former president had entered. He appeared well rested and groomed, he was dressed in a navy suit, of the kind he would have worn while he was still president, of the kind he wore in the photograph. I briefly wondered how he had obtained it, if it was something his legal team organized, if it was off the rack or if they had arranged for a tailor to visit the Detention Center in the middle of the night, as I had several nights ago. His manner was calm and even subdued, and yet I was certain he was aware of how the energy of the Court bent in his direction, toward the black hole of his personality.

Kees was still standing before him with his arms spread wide, although the pose was beginning to wilt, the former president had left him hanging. Uncertainty crossed his face, and I felt suddenly sympathetic. The former president nodded, his manner formal and distant. At this, Kees seemed to recover some of his bluster and he embraced the man enthusiastically, as if they were old friends. The former president withstood this assault of affection. Encouraged, Kees guided him to his seat, keeping one hand on his shoulder. I saw that he was making a point of maintaining physical contact with the former president, and I thought that beyond his own egotism, the gesture was calculated to declare that the accused was a man like any other, a man who could exist within a civil society, who had both friends and a family, and from whom we did not need protection.

As if to demonstrate that he was not afraid. I wondered if that was, if that could possibly be, the case. Kees had seemed to me an outlandish but fundamentally ordinary person, with an ordinary person's prejudices and presuppositions. But if it was true that Kees was not at least a little afraid of the former president, especially given his presumed familiarity with the crimes of which he stood accused, then he would have been an unusual man, either a man of considerable courage or a man subject to cognitive dissonance. As I watched, the former president nodded and Kees continued to speak, producing what must have been a logorrheic stream of language. I tried to imagine what he might have been saying, some technical explanation perhaps. But then I thought probably it did not matter what he was saying, the entire point was the pantomime, the theater, through this little performance Kees was normalizing the accused, before the eyes of the Court and the cameras, before the eyes of the world.

That's the new counsel, Amina said, her voice low. Below, the former president suddenly raised his hands, as if to say enough. Kees immediately stepped back. It was clear that he had been dismissed. He was in the employ of the former president, as a vast number of people once had been. Now that circle had dwindled to the individuals gathered around the accused in the courtroom, Kees was among the last. I thought he would be wise to maintain his caution, in the brief exchange between the two men I had seen the powerful volatility at the core of the former president, no doubt the source of his ability to dominate and intimidate. The former president adjusted his tie, his expression at once pompous and disgruntled. Kees returned to his place behind the table, a moment later the door at the front of the court-room opened and the judges entered.

Will the Court please rise. Chamber I is now in session. Kees rose alongside the others, he lifted his chin and narrowed his eyes, once again his chest seemed to puff outward be-neath his robes. Beside me, Amina had begun to interpret, her hands placed on the desk in front of her, a pen woven between her fingers. She seemed very calm, almost placid in manner. *You may be seated.* Carefully, Amina removed a piece of lint from the sleeve of her blouse and spoke the words of the presiding judge. *I immediately give the floor to the witness.*

A portly, middle-aged man entered the courtroom and went to the witness stand. He lowered himself into the chair with caution, a furtive and hangdog expression on his face. *If you could stand. Please. Yes—if you could please stand and give your date of birth and your current occupation.* The man clam-bered to his feet. The former president adjusted his tie again, I wondered then if this was a nervous tic, rather than a ges-ture of intimidation, I thought I detected a flicker of appre-hension in his eyes. Or perhaps it was anticipation. *Thank you. Please be seated. Yes, thank you. Go ahead.* Amina paused. The witness leaned toward the microphone and looked at the judge.

Good afternoon, Madame. Amina spoke slowly, enunciat-ing each syllable. I could see that she was listening to the witness, adjusting to the patterns of his speech. *Thank you for giving me the floor. I will try to answer your questions to the best of my ability, I would like to be of help.* Amina had quickened her pace, and now she spoke rapidly, occasionally stopping to exhale. *Before we return to the questioning by the prosecution, may I add a few words of my own?* Amina's forehead wrinkled. At the front, the presiding judge nodded wearily. *There is no need for all this theater. It has been nearly five years since my colleague and friend was removed from our country and brought here under entirely false pretenses. Such games of hide-and-seek are not good for the reputation of the Court. Back home, this case has been seen as nothing less than a political kidnapping.* He shook his head. *Back home, they are saying why do they not arrest the current president, this illegitimate president?*

The men and women in the public gallery began to cheer, their voices loud enough to permeate the glass barrier. A woman pumped her fist in the air and clapped her hands, soon that entire section of gallery was following suit. I could see the journalists' attention pivot toward the former president's supporters, the scene would make for a good story. The guards positioned in the aisles of the gallery seemed powerless to stop or even contain the pandemonium. Down below, the former president was smiling, as he raised a hand to his supporters.

Quiet. I must ask for quiet.

The presiding judge shook her head.

Please control your supporters.

The former president's gaze remained fixed on the public gallery. For the first time since entering the courtroom, his face was wide-open, almost vulnerable—there was no hint of triumph, or subterfuge, or strategy in it. He was clearly emotional in the face of his enduring popularity. *I must insist that you control your supporters, or they will be barred from the gallery. Again, I am insisting.* Slowly, reluctantly, he raised both hands and motioned for his supporters to be seated. They quieted immediately, dropping obediently into their seats, their eyes on the former president. He nodded, almost to himself.

The judge peered at him through her spectacles, her expression stern. *May I remind you that there are certain standards of decorum that are expected of visitors to the Court. Should they fail to adhere to those standards, they will immediately be expelled from the Court and denied any further access to these premises.* The former president stared at her unblinkingly. After a moment, she continued, now addressing the witness. *As for you, sir. I must ask that you confine yourself to responding to questions from the prosecution. We are already running behind schedule.* The witness nodded, and as the prosecution began their questioning, the energy seemed to drain from the courtroom.

For the next ninety minutes the prosecution questioned the witness over matters that were at once meandering and

technical in the extreme, during which time both the prosecution and the witness seemed to grow frustrated and weary.
The judges interrupted at various points, largely to urge the
witness and the prosecution alike to be more succinct in their
words and lines of questioning, evidently they were serious
about being behind schedule. In the second half of the session I began to interpret. I was more than usually nervous,
not only because this was a trial of consequence and an error
in interpretation could have considerable effect, but because
I was afraid that Kees might somehow recognize my voice,
unlikely as that might be—we had, I reminded myself, met
only once and spoken barely at all.

Still, when I leaned forward and spoke into the microphone, my voice gave an audible wobble, so that several
of the members of the Court looked up in surprise. I felt
Amina tense beside me. I found my composure soon enough,
to everyone's relief, or at least Amina's, who reached out
and gave my hand a reassuring squeeze. Kees did not respond to the sound of my voice, not even the tremor at the
start. Nevertheless I was relieved when the session came to
an end and the presiding judge rose to her feet.

Almost immediately, the room crawled with movement. The attention, which until that moment had been
focused on the witness and the prosecutor, now atomized,
scattering across the courtroom. Even before the three

judges had exited, people were bending to gather their papers and leaning their heads together to converse. The former president remained at the edge of the room with a security guard at his side, he stood as if he were waiting for something, for someone to come and speak to him perhaps. I looked for Kees, to my surprise he and his colleagues were rapidly making their way toward the exit.

I turned back to the former president. His face, as he watched his counsel disappear through the doors, was thoroughly perplexed. His gaze moved to the public gallery, which was also emptying. His expression tightened. The guard leaned toward him and he nodded. His shoulders slumped and he suddenly appeared much older, I realized it must have taken him great effort to appear before the Court with his posture so erect, his bearing still presidential, to marshal what charisma remained, because contrary to popular belief, charisma was not inherent but had to be constantly reinforced. The former president's performance—for that was what it had been—had left him depleted and now he shuffled toward the exit, head bowed.

Amina looked at me. Well done, she said. She smiled warmly at me. I'm going to the cafeteria to get a cup of tea. As she rose to her feet she placed her hands at the small of her back and grimaced. I asked if she was okay, then said that I would accompany her, I was also in need of a coffee. That was relatively easy, she continued as we made our way downstairs, even with that display in the gallery. There's always something. The lobby was full of school groups and visitors and as we made our way across, I said to Amina that I had once met the new defense counsel. She turned to look at me, puzzled. Where? Here? As we joined the line at the cafeteria, I said, No. At a party, by chance. Ah, she said. So it's not as if you are in the same social circle. Would that be a problem? I asked. She paused. No, I don't think so. But be careful. They say he is very good at his job. We had reached the front of the line, and she said, Let me get this. What would you like?

9.

Several days later, I was called into a meeting with the defense. It was a Friday, one of the days when the Court was not in session. I was in the office with Amina when Bettina's assistant rushed over, she wore an expression of consternation, and I asked if something had happened. Nothing serious, she said, don't worry. It's only that the defense requires an interpreter, and you have been specifically requested. I was startled. Why? I asked. Why me? She shook her head, she didn't know, but Bettina had told her to accommodate the request. When? I asked. Now, she said, you need to go immediately.

I gathered my things and pulled on my coat. It had been a week since Adriaan had gone, a week of staying in the apartment alone. Each night I returned to the house, climbing the stairs to the second floor, slipping the key into the lock, opening the door. And each time I entered and hung up my coat, I felt a throb of happiness so pronounced it frightened me. I had returned to my own apartment only once, to pack a bag of clothes that I ferried back to Adriaan's. Dimly, I understood that I could be happy there, notwithstanding its complications, for example the photograph of Gaby that still rested on the shelf.

As for Adriaan himself, he sent me a message one day after his departure, asking if I was in the apartment and if everything was okay. I texted back to say that I was there and very happy. He wrote back to say that he was pleased, and that it was hot in Lisbon. Immediately I imagined Adriaan, with the children and with Gaby, his phone vibrating as he received my text, I saw him checking the screen surreptitiously as they sat in an outdoor café. Gaby turning idly to ask, Who's that? The idea made me somehow feel ashamed. But that feeling did not keep me from waiting for his messages, for the texts and emails that followed, detailing some event or another, or expressing the warmth of his feelings toward me. Those small missives anchored me to the apartment, although it is also true that I wondered why he never picked up the telephone and called.

Nor had he made any reference to the date of his return, *It will only be a week, or possibly a little longer.* That week had now passed. I left the Court and walked in the rain to the nearest stop and took the bus to the Detention Center, where I relinquished my bag to the security guard and was taken to a conference room. I followed the attendant up a flight of stairs and down a corridor, she stopped at a metal door, nodding to the guard who sat posted outside. He rose to his feet and knocked. Come in, a voice said almost immediately, and then the guard opened the door and motioned for me to enter.

I was greeted with a scene that had the formality of a Renaissance tableau. Several men sat at a conference table covered with papers, while the former president stood to one side. His gaze trained upon me as I stood in the doorway. The entire legal team appeared to be present, or a good proportion of them anyway, including Kees, who watched me as I came in and whose expression disclosed nothing, not a trace of recognition. A CCTV camera was suspended in the corner, the glossy eye recording everything. Behind me, the door swung shut.

After a long moment, during which I wondered if I had been summoned accidentally, as it seemed clear that no one in this room had any real need of me, entrenched as they already were in the session, the former president spoke. Thank you for coming, he said in French. I saw one of the men sitting at the table look up at Kees, who stood across the room from the former president. One of the lawyers cleared his throat and asked me to sit down. He poured a glass of water, as I reached for it I realized that I was flushed. I took a sip. When I lowered the glass, I saw that Kees was still watching me. His expression was neutral and I quickly turned my face away.

Slowly, the former president approached and sat down in the chair beside me. He was dressed in a polo shirt and slacks and had tied a maroon-colored sweater around his neck, as if he were at the country club. He leaned toward me conspiratorially, and nodding to Kees, said, His French is terrible, much worse than he thinks. I didn't respond. He cleared his throat and said to the room at large, Let's continue. One of the lawyers began. His speech was what the English called cut glass, and not too rapid, from that point of view the task of interpretation was easy. *The thing to keep in mind is that the trial might continue for months, years. The narrative of a trial functions differently in a case like this. It is not as simple as telling a persuasive story.* I sat beside the former president, directing my words into his ear, reaching for a legal pad and pen. He leaned back in his chair, his gaze resting on the lawyer whose words I spoke.

Remember that the judges are themselves aware of how a story fluctuates over the course of years—the trial moves from one side to the other, the story changes, and memory is unreliable. It's impossible to retain the pattern of these shifts. The advantage can all too easily go to the side that achieves momentum in the final hour. The lawyer paused. *As a result, there are safeguards in place, which present both danger and opportunity. At the end of each day, a record is produced. Those records are collated and together are of utmost importance to the trial.*

He looked around the room. *As much as it may be our instinct to create a persuasive narrative across the days and weeks and months of the trial, we will not win unless we keep our eye on what happens on a day-to-day level. Strategy and tactics are necessary. And so as much*—and here he looked directly at the former president—*as it is critical to focus on the big picture, as much as we may wish to focus on the story that is told outside the walls of the courtroom, we must proceed with this daily record in mind. Our victory or our loss is in that record. Not in the*—*performance, shall we say, of our most recent witness, which, however gratifying it may have been on a personal level, did nothing for our case.*

He cleared his throat and picked up a file as he waited for me to finish. Beside me, the former president was perfectly still. I was close enough to observe the texture of his skin, the particularities of his features, I could smell the scent of the soap he must have used that morning. He did not move as I spoke into his ear, as quickly and discreetly as possible, I was aware of the whole room waiting. I thought how different this mode of interpretation was to the work performed in the booth, where we were called upon to speak clearly and enunciate every word for the sake of the public, for the sake of the record. Here, I spoke in murmurs and whispers, there was something underhanded about the communication. I quickly finished and was silent.

I could not tell what the former president was feeling, whether he had accepted or even understood the lawyer's somewhat technical and certainly counterintuitive advice, the Court appeared at first and even second glance as a venue designed for narrative persuasion. The former president gave no indication either way, and after a moment, the lawyer continued. There followed another highly technical discussion, the content of which was obscure at best and as the minutes stretched onward, I began to lose track of what was actually under discussion.

This was not aided by the fact that interpretation can be profoundly disorienting, you can be so caught up in the minutiae of the act, in trying to maintain utmost fidelity to the words being spoken first by the subject and then by yourself, that you do not necessarily apprehend the sense of the sentences themselves: you literally do not know what you are saying. Language loses its meaning. This was happening to me now, in the conference room. I was absorbed by the task at hand, of decoding the legalese in which the content of the discussion was encased, so securely that nothing seemed to penetrate and nothing escaped. And yet—as I stared down at the pad of paper in front of me, covered in shorthand—something did seep out. I saw the words I had been saying, for nearly twenty minutes now, *cross-border raid, mass grave, armed youth.*

I reached for the glass of water. One of the junior associates was speaking now—a solid wall of language that barreled toward me as I drank all the water in the glass, poured another, and then drank that. I set the glass down, I had lost my place, I looked down at the notepad again, as if I would find a clue there. The associate came to an abrupt stop, the former president turned to look at me. Is everything okay, the associate asked sharply. I just need a moment, I said. Could we go back—the associate answered impatiently, Yes, yes, of course. How far? He exchanged glances with Kees, who was watching me, one arm folded over the other. He had been silent the entire time, now he suddenly spoke. Let's take a break. Five minutes? And the others immediately rose to their feet as if they too had only been waiting for an excuse to pause.

To my surprise, the former president also rose and headed out of the room with the others, he seemed entirely at liberty. I watched him go. I remained seated, although I could have used some air, perhaps even more than the others. The room was nearly empty when I realized that Kees was still in the room, he alone had stayed behind. He approached and stood before me. I know you came here on short notice and I'm grateful, he said. I nodded, I was wary, his tone was indeterminate, stubbornly ambiguous, it was true that his manner was familiar, but there was no concrete sign of recognition in his manner or in any of the words he said. I might have asked him any number of questions or even brought up the issue myself, but the situation was far from neutral. Kees was in a position of considerable power, all it would take was one complaint and my contract would be, if not terminated, then surely not extended.

He likes you, Kees said suddenly. It's almost as if he finds your presence soothing. I tried not to flinch, I was aware that Kees was observing me closely. Various words flashed into my mind again—*perpetrator, ride-through, ethnic cleansing*. But that's not the only reason why it's useful for us to have you here, Kees continued. He folded his arms and stared at the floor. Your reaction helps us understand what the emotional effect of the evidence and the testimony is likely to be. To some extent we are too inured. He gestured to the papers spread across the table with one hand. Even as we must concern ourselves with technicalities, it is important to remember the emotional component. Your response is a good reminder of how volatile the feelings around a case like this are.

He pronounced the word *feelings* with light but definite contempt. Kees looked at me. You know, he continued, and now there was a faint smile on his lips, you look very familiar, have we met? I was silent as he came closer. He sat down on the edge of the conference table, his legs angled toward me, his body mere inches away. I wondered how many times he had performed these exact moves, the effect was at once brazen and impersonal. I was increasingly certain that he did not remember me, and that he had made the same approach to many hundreds of women, *Have we met?* I heard a noise outside in the corridor and turned to look, voices approached and then faded again, it was only some people walking by.

But it had been enough, Kees abruptly rose to his feet and walked back to the other side of the conference table. His manner had changed, he flipped through his papers with a frown. I was about to get up when he looked across the table and suddenly said, Do you see much of Adriaan? There was nothing particular in the words themselves or the way he pronounced them, although perhaps the casual manner was overdone. But even before I looked up I knew I would find some small sliver of malice in his gaze, and when our eyes met it was there, it must have always been there. At that moment, the others filed in and before I could respond, Kees snapped his head back down to his papers. He made a sound of mild irritation, then looked up and said sharply, Come in, please. We're running behind. Let's not waste any more time.

The former president sat down beside me. He nodded to me and I nodded back. The former president sighed, then rubbed his face with one hand. He turned to me and asked in his calm and euphonious French, Are you okay with all this? He gestured to the table, perhaps to the room at large, his eyes fell on my legal pad and the words scribbled on its pages, words that he couldn't possibly have made out given their script and shorthand, but whose contents he knew all too well. He winced, as if embarrassed, and then made an oddly pleading gesture with his hands. It's a lot, I know. It looks much worse than it really is, the language has no nuance. He frowned, his eyes still on the legal pad. One word—*perpetrator*—for such a range of acts, performed for such a range of reasons.

He shook his head and sighed. Of course, I don't need to tell you this, he continued. This is your stock in trade, you deal with words. The others in the room were talking quietly or looking through their papers. He was waiting for me to respond. I hesitated and then said, My job is to make the space between languages as small as possible. This was not the rebuke I wished to make, as a statement it was abstract to the point of saying almost nothing at all. And yet it was true: I would not obfuscate the meaning of what he had done, of these words that he deemed so insufficient, my job was to ensure that there would be no escape route between languages.

The former president was still, he appeared to be waiting for me to continue. But I would not say anything more, and at last the former president looked at Kees and he said, reluctantly, wearily, Well. Shall we continue? And I finally understood that he was bored, bored by the recitation of his own crimes, bored by the fashioning of a legal strategy that might yet free him. He surveyed the lawyers around the table, he could not bear them because they were the physical manifestation of his culpability, of which I had little doubt. These men who hectored him about the specificities of his actions, he wished to be free of them, in the same way that he wished to be free of his guilt.

This was why he found my presence soothing. Not because he required my interpretation, not even because I was an amusing distraction, but because he wished for someone to be present during those long hours, someone who would not insist on examining the actions of his past, from which there could no longer be any escape. And I realized that for him I was pure instrument, someone without will or judgment, a consciousness-free zone into which he could escape, the only company he could now bear—that, that was the reason why he had requested my presence, that was the reason I was there. I wanted to get up and leave the room, to explain that there had been some mistake. I saw myself doing it. But that was only in my head. That was not what actually happened. What actually took place was that I remained in my seat, that I interpreted for the former president, that I remained there, in that room with those men, until they no longer wanted me.

10.

Jana's opening at the Mauritshuis was more than usually crowded, perhaps due to the theme of the exhibition, one that was both serious and tongue in cheek. Jana had frequently spoken about the pressure to achieve better attendance numbers, to find ways of reframing the permanent collection so that it appealed to a younger and broader audience.

It was with this directive in mind that Jana had conceived the current exhibition, which was titled *Slow Food* and was the museum's first exhibition devoted to still-life paintings of food. Jana admitted the concept and the title in particular were something of a gimmick, entirely different to the first two exhibitions she had overseen. But she insisted that she had found plenty of merit in the idea. It's a clear theme in Golden Age painting, a definite genre, she said, even if titles like *Still Life with Cheeses, Almonds and Pretzels* do make you think of a Jeff Koons sculpture. I suppose that's interesting in and of itself. There is a lot to be said about class and consumption and the culture of display.

I looked at the people gathered in the museum lobby, dressed in designer brands and playing ostentatiously with their smartphones. They drank their wine and stood around the bust of Johan Maurits, who founded the museum with a fortune built from the transatlantic slave trade and the expansion of Dutch Brazil, Jana had told me the history on a previous visit. She wished they would take the bust down, not only did it celebrate a slave trader and colonialist, it wasn't even a good piece of art. I had to agree, I thought Maurits appeared particularly pompous in this rendering by Bartholomeus Eggers, with his jowls and pursed lips and ornate dress. He stared into space, one hand splayed across his front. Although the bust was surrounded by guests, no one seemed to pay it any mind, the history present but unconsidered. As I watched, a man in a suit yawned and brushed against the bust before lazily righting himself again.

I went upstairs, where I saw Jana on the far side of the gallery, deep in conversation with two women with perfectly coiffed blond hair, they were both wearing suits and high heels, as if they had arrived directly from the office. The quality of Jana's attention seemed to suggest that they were donors, she was nodding enthusiastically but her smile was stiff and hollow. I didn't want to interrupt and instead went into the next gallery, which housed the permanent collection. The room was empty, and I wandered undisturbed, the sounds of the crowd receding as I passed through.

The rooms at the Mauritshuis were small in scale, galleries that felt almost domestic compared to the exhibition spaces at some museums, their size so immense they seemed to force an experience of sublimity upon the visitor. I thought that I preferred the intimacy of these rooms, which were better suited to the paintings not only because of the size of the works—some were no bigger than a sheet of paper, the kind of paintings you wanted to approach, that could not be experienced at a distance—but also because of their subject matter. Unlike the paintings in Jana's exhibition, the canvases in this room primarily featured figures, men and women and children.

The artifice of their poses was evident, but that did not detract from the intimacy of the paintings—in fact it was the very act of posing, the relationship that act implied, that created this sense of uncanny familiarity. In some cases they were clearly posing for the painter, they gazed into what I thought of as the lens or camera eye, although of course the concept was an anachronism, they would have been gazing not into an apparatus but directly at the painter himself. The idea was almost impossibly personal, and I realized the notion of such a sustained human gaze was outside the realm of experience today.

For that reason, the paintings opened up a dimension that you did not normally see in photographs, in these paintings you could feel the weight of time passing. I thought that was why, as I stood before a painting of a young girl in half-light, there was something that was both guarded and vulnerable in her gaze. It was not the contradiction of a single instant, but rather it was as if the painter had caught her in two separate states of emotion, two different moods, and managed to contain them within the single image. There would have been a multitude of such instants captured in the canvas, between the time she first sat down before the painter and the time she rose, neck and upper body stiff, from the final sitting. That layering—in effect a kind of temporal blurring, or simultaneity—was perhaps ultimately what distinguished painting from photography. I wondered if that was the reason why contemporary painting seemed to me so much flatter, to lack the mysterious depth of these works, because so many painters now worked from photographs.

I moved to the next painting, which depicted a young woman seated beside a table, her face illuminated by the flame from a candle—her broad forehead and rounded cheeks bathed in golden light, the crisp folds of her white blouse almost blinding. The painter's use of chiaroscuro was particularly striking, at least to my inexpert eye—I could not describe its precise characteristics, I knew only that it was as if the light had been rendered three-dimensional, extending past the frame of the painting, until the canvas itself seemed to be the source of illumination. A man stood behind the young woman, leaning against the table in a pose that was casual and raffish, somehow off-putting, he seemed to infringe upon her personal space, although *personal space* was not a phrase that could have occurred to the young woman, another anachronism.

I stepped closer to the painting. The young woman—girl, really—was working a piece of embroidery, some small domestic task that seemed of unlikely interest to the young man in his Cossack hat and tunic. He leered down at her, it was obviously not the task but rather the young girl herself who had caught his attention. She was in white, he was in black, the symbolism was clear enough but the exact nature of the encounter was opaque to me. I peered at the title card—the titles of these paintings were usually descriptive and never very poetic, they had none of the forced obscurity of contemporary art titles. The work was called *Man Offering Money to a Young Woman.*

I looked back at the painting, this time I saw that the man appeared to be holding coins in the palm of his cupped hand. The palm was discreetly proffered, with the other hand he was gently pulling at her arm, as if to turn her away from her work and toward the proposition before her. I saw the uncommon skill with which the artist had communicated the subtleties of force and resistance—the drama in the pull of his hand on her arm, the stiffness of her posture, the fearful widening of the eyes.

But the true tension in the painting lay not in the perfect consistency with which that moment of contact had been rendered, but rather in the inconsistency at the heart of the image. No matter how long I stared at the painting, I could not reconcile the perfect modesty of the young woman, whose entire body was covered apart from her face and hands, with the lascivious manner and offer being made by the man. Perhaps he was simply offering to purchase the embroidered cloth? But if so, then why the expression of fear on the young woman's face? Why the young woman's concentration, so brittle and freighted with meaning, as if it were the only rebuff she was permitted to make?

I looked at the title card again, to my surprise I saw that the painting had been made by a woman, Judith Leyster. I had never heard of her, but I knew it was unusual for a woman to achieve recognition during the Golden Age, even now it was rare for a female painter to reach the stature of her male colleagues. According to the card, Leyster was born in 1609. The painting was dated 1631: she was only twenty-two years old when she had made it. It seemed miraculous that the painting had been made by someone in her very early twenties, it was not only the technical skill that was striking—but that was also extraordinary, to achieve that level of mastery at such a young age—it was the ambiguity of the image itself.

I turned back to the canvas, and it occurred to me then that only a woman could have made this image. This was not a painting of temptation, but rather one of harassment and intimidation, a scene that could be taking place right now in nearly anyplace in the world. The painting operated around a schism, it represented two irreconcilable subjective positions: the man, who believed the scene to be one of ardor and seduction, and the woman, who had been plunged into a state of fear and humiliation. That schism, I now realized, was the true inconsistency animating the canvas, and the true object of Leyster's gaze.

There you are. Startled, I turned. I had been so absorbed in the painting that I had not heard the sound of footfalls in the gallery. Jana stood in front of me. We hadn't seen each other since we had met for dinner with Adriaan, over a month ago. She had been preoccupied with the exhibition, and although I had sent her several messages I had not heard from her until she called to insist that I attend the opening and the dinner after, her manner charming and blunt as ever. I told her I would be there, I had been missing Jana's company and wanted to discuss Adriaan with her. Things had gone awry in the past month, and I had felt the shape and meaning of his absence begin to change.

The week had extended to two without explanation or anything more than the briefest of apologies. I was already feeling vulnerable when my disquiet was sharply compounded by another encounter with Kees. Less than a week after my first session with the former president, I was called into another meeting with the defense. The meeting itself passed without incident, but as I left the conference room Kees hurried down the corridor after me. As soon as he reached me he slowed to a walk, an expression of mild surprise on his face, as if he had happened upon me by chance and we had not just spent several hours together. Instinctively, I began walking a little faster. He kept pace beside me until I stopped and turned to face him, exasperated.

I only wanted to ask how you were, he said. He sounded affronted, and immediately I was made to feel as if I were overreacting. He clasped his hands together in a manner that was unnatural and then a little threatening. I imagine this is difficult for you.

It's fine, I said curtly.

Is it? But perhaps you are right. He paused, eyes scanning my face avidly. Adriaan is unlikely to succeed. Gaby is very wrapped up in this new man of hers.

It was as if I had taken a blow to the chest. I don't think I understand, I said.

Understand what? It's as I said. He won't win her back.

But he's—

What, still in love with her? It certainly is a gesture, rushing off to Portugal. Gaby called me that very evening, she found the entire thing quite irrational and inconvenient, it seems her new man is prone to fits of jealousy. I recoiled a little as he repeated the phrase *new man*, his voice salacious and excitable. He shook his head and waggled his finger at me. He's thrown a spanner in the works, our friend Adriaan, turning up as he has. And of course the children— he trailed off, evidently the children were a matter too pedestrian to be discussed.

I suppose the children must be happy to see him, I said. My mouth was dry, my words cold and halting.

Yes, well—children are, aren't they? He rushed on, despite the fact that his words made little sense. But enough about Adriaan, he said with a grin as he lurched in my direction. I wondered if I could take you for a drink?

I was both deadened and amazed by the man's audacity, his technique was remarkably repetitive, it was the same strategy every time, he capitalized on disorientation. The entire thing was so threadbare and at the same time it was not ineffective, I did find myself disoriented, if not in the way he hoped. I excused myself and hurried out of the building, collecting my bag from the security guard. I took out my phone and texted Adriaan, *Are you okay?* He wrote back at once, *Yes, fine.* And then nothing further.

I didn't know what to do, still less what to believe. Adriaan had already told me that things with Gaby were complicated and as the days became weeks and now a full month it had of course occurred to me that the situation between them was becoming more rather than less entrenched. Was it possible that he had changed his mind? Wasn't it possible that he had told me something less than the truth? This was not what I had hoped, I was now aware that I was in a precarious position. Had Jana asked me then how things were with Adriaan, I might have told her any number of things: that I didn't really know, that I had moved into his apartment, that the entire thing was on the verge of fizzling out or close enough.

But she didn't ask, at least not in that particular moment. She was accompanied by an elegant woman I did not recognize, stylishly dressed, the kind of woman I might have surreptitiously admired in the street. This is Eline, Jana said, I wanted you to meet. The woman smiled as she took my hand and although I was distracted I felt at once that I liked her. Were you very bored? Jana asked. I shook my head, No, I only became preoccupied with this painting, I pointed to the Leyster and said, Somehow I had never noticed it before.

The Proposition, Jana said. As it's usually called. It's a beautiful piece. Leyster was a singular case—she was one of the first women in the Guild, and she achieved some renown during her lifetime. But after her death many of her paintings were misattributed, it was only at the end of the nineteenth century that the error was corrected. And then? I asked. Jana shrugged. Well, her paintings are here. I suppose she has some reputation, though it's still less than she deserves. I nodded, I saw that Eline was also examining the painting. Are you done? I asked Jana, and she shook her head, No, I need to go back. But you're staying for the dinner? I nodded, Jana was already retreating, I saw that she had wanted to introduce Eline to me in part so that we would each have the other to speak to.

Jana has a gift for friendship, Eline said. She insists upon it. We both laughed. Her words were gentle but forthright and there was an immediate ease between us. In the brief pause that followed, I realized that Jana had left without establishing any common ground between us, I knew nothing about the woman who stood beside me. As we began walking, Eline indicated the paintings in the gallery. They have such an air of perfect tranquility, but it was not a period without upheaval. The Dutch Empire was rapidly expanding, in many ways these paintings have to be read in that context. The relentless domesticity of these quiet interiors takes on a different meaning seen in that light, she said. It means something, to face inward, to turn your back on the storm brewing outside.

I said that she seemed to know a great deal about the period, and she smiled. I'm an art historian, I teach at the university. It's surprising that I didn't meet Jana earlier, The Hague is such a small place and its art world even smaller, but I suppose she hasn't been here so long. I was of course aware of her appointment, she added. As we continued through the galleries, slowly returning to Jana's exhibition, I asked her what she thought of the show. She's done an excellent job, Eline said. Of the exhibition and of the position as a whole. It's not an easy thing, what she's being asked to do. She needs to modernize the institution, but she also needs to keep us art historians satisfied. I asked if that was how they met and she said, No, we met in another way altogether, it was quite unexpected. She didn't say anything further, and I didn't feel that I could press her, there were any number of ways the two of them might have met, as she had said, The Hague was a small place.

We had reached the exhibition space, which was rapidly emptying out. An usher approached and asked if we were attending the dinner, and if so, could we please make our way downstairs. Eline and I looked at each other, Jana was nowhere in sight, and after a moment we went down to the museum lobby, where an elaborate scene had been produced. There were long banquet tables covered in white cloth. At various stations around the lobby they had set up spreads of food in perfect imitation of the paintings in the exhibition.

It's like an inversion of Zeuxis and Parrhasius, Eline said with an amused smile. I tried to recall the specifics of the reference, something that I had learned in school, a story about a contest to determine the best painter in ancient Greece. I remembered that Zeuxis created a painting of grapes so realistic that birds swept down to peck at the panel. That was only half the story, and I couldn't remember what followed, what the rival painter Parrhasius had produced. The image of the birds swooping down through the crowd, their wings beating upon the panel, had subsumed the rest of the narrative. In any case, as Eline had said the scene in the lobby was certainly a perfect inversion of the painting Zeuxis had made, they had even set up frames around each tableau, through which guests were invited to reach, in order to take a piece of cheese or a leg of meat or indeed to pluck a grape.

I was sure Jana must be pleased, it was an impressive, even ostentatious, display. The room was crowded with delighted guests, the noise and chatter of their appreciation. Jana appeared behind us at that moment, slinging an arm around my shoulder, and asked what we thought. Eline said at once that it was wonderful, and Jana said that they had commissioned a food artist to make the dioramas, a young woman who had studied at the Rijksakademie and was now getting commissions from all the big biennials. She was whisked away before she could continue, I saw that she was animated by the success of the evening. There was no formal seating plan, instead there was a towering stack of plates piled on a table set in the middle of the lobby. Guests were crowding around the paintings, plates in hand, sawing away at sides of meat and cheese wheels through the various picture frames, the entire scene was bizarre and amusing.

I thought of Adriaan, it occurred to me that this was the world he had inhabited with Gaby. They would have circulated through this room with ease, I was sure that between them they would have known most of the people in attendance, in some ways it was their world even more than it was Jana's. I felt a rush of fear crowd into me. I was not of this place. I had an image of Adriaan, together with Gaby again, for a moment it was as if they were there in the room. Around us, lines were forming. Shall we? Eline asked gently, as if aware of my distraction. I like the look of that Clara Peeters.

She indicated a display of cheeses and said with a laugh, I think our dinner will consist of cheese and bread, the fish and lobster have already been depleted. It was true, happy diners were now sitting down at the banquet tables, their plates heavy with food. Servers circulated with pitchers of wine, everything had been thought of. We joined the line and then reached through the frame to cut slices of cheese. Eline took an apple and some other fruit from another display, It is wonderfully executed, she murmured as she bit into a peach and surveyed the scene. If you look, the lighting has been adjusted to mimic the paintings. She gestured to the lighting rig above. Even the wreckage is somehow funny and interesting, you never get to see the paintings in this state.

A while later, Jana joined us. She sat down in the chair next to me and slipped her heels off. What a night, she said. She sounded tired, the words a little ambiguous, the evening might have been a success or a disaster in her eyes. Eline said, It's wonderful, you must be very pleased. Jana leaned forward eagerly. What did you think of the exhibition? she asked. Eline reached for Jana's hands and grasped them in her own, It's a triumph. There was a great deal of kindness in her voice, and although I did not doubt the sincerity of her words, I could see she was aware of how much they meant to Jana. Jana nodded as if relieved, and a little later Eline stood up and said that she needed to go. It was such a pleasure to meet you, she said to me, and although the words were mere convention, I again felt she meant them. Can we meet again? she said, and Jana immediately said that she would put us in touch.

Eline smiled and said good night. As she watched her go, Jana yawned, the crowd was beginning to disperse and it was as if she had officially clocked off, she reached for her glass of wine. Isn't she lovely? Did you like her? she asked. Very much, I said. How did you meet?

She was in front of my building.

What do you mean?

Her brother was the man who was attacked—you remember, in that mugging last month.

I looked at her, startled.

She didn't tell you? Jana drank from her glass. That's how we met, she was standing in front of the apartment building, maybe one week after the attack. It was so clear she didn't belong there, I thought she was lost, or I don't know what, but for some reason I stopped and asked if she was okay. She looked at me and then she burst into tears. We went to the café around the corner and she told me what had happened, that her brother had been attacked and beaten while in the neighborhood, that he had been hospitalized for over a week.

Jana reached over and squeezed my hand, her manner warm and affectionate. You know, I'm sorry not to have been in touch. The exhibition has taken up all my time.

But he's fine? I asked. Her brother?

Eline's brother? I think so, she said with a shrug. Although I don't think there's been much progress in the case.

He can't remember anything. He doesn't even know why he was in the neighborhood, or what he came there to do. It's a total mystery.

A waiter was moving through what remained of the crowd, distributing plates of seedcake. Jana took two plates and handed me one. She began eating, she must have been very hungry. How is Adriaan? she asked between bites. She wasn't looking at me as she spoke, but there was nothing false about the casual way in which she asked the question, she was too tired to be self-conscious. I thought he was very nice, she said, and her manner was so matter-of-fact that I wondered if I had imagined it all, the complicity and the flirtation. He seemed kind. Which is a rarity. She took another bite and then looked at me. Don't you think? I nodded. I didn't say anything further. But I believed her words to be true. Later that evening, I sent Adriaan a message, I asked when he would return, and then I asked how things were with Gaby, where things stood with his marriage.

11.

Adriaan did not reply to the message. A day passed, and after I reached for my phone yet again in the hopes of having received a reply, I lowered it and looked around me. I had been living in Adriaan's apartment for over a month and yet I had changed almost nothing inside it. I realized I had been trying to occupy the apartment in as discreet a manner as possible, as if to illustrate to Adriaan upon his return how easily I would slip into the fabric of his life, how little disturbance I would cause. To understand this was humiliating. I was a woman waiting for a lover, dressed in obscene lingerie, body arrayed on the bed in a pose of hopeful seduction.

I felt sudden and real anger toward Adriaan, who had placed me in this absurd position, who had asked me to live in his apartment, had promised to return in a week, only to abscond into silence. It was not that I had never before experienced an unexpected silence from a man, but I would not have expected that from Adriaan. I placed the phone on the table, I looked around again, nothing had changed in the apartment, with the exception of the volume I had purchased at Anton de Rijk's shop in the Old Town. I had been complicit in my own erasure.

I picked up the book, this history on The Hague, and held it in my hand. I saw the volume now for what it was, the artifact of a brief moment when I thought I might yet have a place in Adriaan's city. I threw the book hard across the room. The burn of humiliation remained in my throat all day, and by the following day I felt deflated and worn out. I had made myself too easy to leave, stashed away like a spare part, I had asked for too little, and now it was too late. That feeling was with me still when I received an email from Jana, a few days later, addressed to both Eline and myself. It was obvious that we should be friends, she wrote, and she was putting us in touch.

I scrolled down the email chain and saw that it was Eline who had written first, congratulating Jana again on the success of the exhibition and saying how much she had enjoyed meeting me. I felt flattered, I remembered how I had liked Eline, and I wrote back at once. I wanted to be taken out of my own thoughts, away from the entire impossible situation. We arranged to meet at a café close to Adriaan's apartment. As I entered, it occurred to me that she might ask if I lived in the area, and I did not know what I would say. Happily, that feeling of uncertainty dissipated as soon as I saw her. She was sitting at a table by the window and in daylight she seemed more delicate than she had at the Mauritshuis, her skin even paler. There were lines around her eyes that I had not noticed before, she was likely older than I had first thought.

As I sat down opposite her, I was conscious again of her brother, Anton de Rijk, like a prickling in the skin. He was a man I had never seen but of whom I had been aware for some time, and whose phantom image she now seemed to summon. She was drinking a cup of herbal tea, she said that of late she had been having trouble sleeping. I nodded. I thought it was likely because of her brother, and it occurred to me that if I asked her why her sleep was so troubled she might even tell me, about the assault, about her brother's physical health.

After a moment, I asked, Is it something in particular? As I asked the question I glanced around the café, as if looking for the waiter, to keep the query from gathering weight. She shook her head. I have a touch of insomnia, it's been that way for years, even when I was a child I was an insomniac. I looked back at her, she was smiling as she spoke. I could never sleep in my own bed, she continued. I would crawl into bed with my parents, I would sleep on the floor in the sitting room, one time my parents found me sleeping on the kitchen counter. She laughed and took a sip of her tea. That no longer happens, thank goodness. But I do all the usual things, I take the necessary precautions. No caffeine after noon, no screens in the bedroom.

She paused. You haven't even ordered, I apologize. She raised her hand and the waiter came to the table. I ordered a coffee, despite my own trouble sleeping, which had redoubled with Adriaan's recent silence. After the waiter left, she said, Jana told me you've been here less than a year, that you've put the city on probation. We both laughed, the invocation of Jana's name furthered our ease. How are we doing, she asked, will you stay? Possibly, I said, if my contract is extended. I didn't say anything about Adriaan.

Where is home?

My family's now in Singapore. Before that I lived in New York.

She nodded. And you enjoy the work?

It's not without complication, I said, and I thought of the former president. The other interpreters had taken to calling me his favorite; it was and it was not a joke. I'd realized that to the others it was a matter of recognition and even distinction, being requested by the accused in this fashion. That such attention could be considered desirable was troubling, it changed the way I saw my colleagues, the register of our interactions in the office, the small talk we made over lunch.

In and of themselves, the sessions with the defense could be exceedingly dull, notwithstanding the tension inside the room, again and again I had the sense that the former president was bored, that he was not hearing the words as I spoke them, that he was barely listening at all. I began to wonder if, rather than bringing home the nature of the acts he had committed, this process was causing them to recede further and further into some state of unreality. The question of his innocence or guilt seemed of little interest to the people in the room, instead they spoke of degrees and framing and context.

In those moments, in the face of the former president's resolute indifference, in that small, airless conference room amidst the folders and piles of paper, something yawned open inside me. The depersonalized nature of the task—I was only an instrument, and during the hours that I was there I was almost never spoken to directly, in fact the only person who bothered to address me at all was the former president—sat alongside the strange intimacy of the encounter, the entire thing was a paradox, impossible to reconcile. Despite the uniformity of these meetings, each time I approached the room with trepidation, and each time I felt I did not know what waited on the other side of the closed door. As for Kees, he never again acknowledged our past acquaintance or the exchange in the corridor, he never even seemed to look at me—he too behaved as if I were not there.

Eline was still waiting for me to respond.

It can be challenging—emotionally, I mean.

Yes, she said. You must be exposed to terrible things, I can't imagine.

At a certain point you no longer understand the words you are saying. I get lost—I'm so focused on the minutiae of the session that I lose track of the larger story. I couldn't tell you at the end of a session what's taken place or what's actually been said.

The waiter placed a cup of coffee before me.

Did you ever see that movie, the one about the interpreter? Eline said once he had moved away. The plot twist is that she's actually a revolutionary. Or not a revolutionary, but the lover of a revolutionary? It was a little hard to follow. On the whole, it didn't make much of an impression on me. But I do remember thinking, what clarity! By the end the actress is waving a gun around, all ambiguity has fallen away, she knows what she has to do. She paused and smiled. You don't have a gun, do you?

I shook my head. No gun. Nor clarity, for that matter.

She laughed. That's probably for the best. My older son loved the movie, I think he has a crush on the actress, she's very beautiful. I asked how old her children were and she said, Ten and twelve. It's gone quickly, their childhood, but it's also gone very slowly. When they are young, it is exhausting and you have no time for yourself, but you can still make them happy. That's no longer the case with my boys. They're old enough to understand things, they see the world as it is. They are wiser but they are also more vulnerable.

As she spoke, I thought of the violence that had entered their lives when her brother was attacked, violence that was not contained on their tablets or phone screens, that was not abstract but fully realized. They were ten and twelve, it was true that by that age many children had already confronted death in some form, a grandmother or a grandfather or a family friend. But death is abstract, even grown men and women can be incapable of understanding it. Violence was something different, violence was easier to comprehend, it existed within the realm of the imagination.

We live in strange times and there is a great deal to worry about, she said abruptly. For one, the possible demise of the European project. I nodded, the date of the Brexit referendum was rapidly approaching, and the polls indicated that against all logic, the UK might well vote to leave the EU. Even the possibility was disturbing, it said nothing good about the world we were living in, or the longevity of institutions such as the Court; nor did it bode well for the upcoming election in the United States. I knew that a Leave vote would be profoundly disorienting for my European friends and colleagues. Jana was especially troubled, she had told me that if the UK voted to leave, it would be impossible for her to return to England, it would no longer be the country she had once known.

I'm worried about the Dutch election next year, this country has a reputation for tolerance but peel back the skin of it— Eline paused. Given the general tendency, I am not optimistic.

It must be difficult for you to explain to the children, I said.

Yes. Their father is useless, he is worse than useless. He's absolutely brutal with them, he doesn't seem to understand that they are still children, that there is a limit to what they can comprehend. Her voice was bitter, she looked across the table at me. I'm divorced, of course. Their father lives in Amsterdam.

But the children live with you?

They go to see him every other weekend. He travels a great deal for work, so those weekends don't happen as regularly as they should. Luckily, my brother and his wife also live in The Hague. She paused, her phone pinged and she picked it up. Her attention moved away from me and I felt the negative space of its absence. She looked up and said that she would need to be going, her son had just texted. His ride has fallen through, I need to go and pick him up.

I nodded, I found that I was disappointed, although I was uncertain of the precise source of my disappointment— was it because she would be leaving when we had only just begun talking, or was it because she had yet to tell me anything of her brother, Anton, or was it simply because I would soon be left alone, and to my own devices? Of course, I murmured. She took out her wallet and placed a bill on the table. As I reached for my bag, she held her hand up. Please, she said, it's a coffee. She stood and waited for me to follow. We divorced a long time ago, she continued as we made our way toward the door. In fact it happened when I was pregnant with my younger son. Her voice was calm and untroubled, it was clear she was speaking of a drama that had long since been resolved. Of course it's important for the boys to know their father, but in many ways their uncle is the primary male presence in their lives, and his wife is more than an aunt to them.

I hesitated, and then said, You're lucky to be so close to your brother. I thought she paused for a moment before she pushed the door open and turned to face me. We're twins, she said. She didn't say anything else, and I walked with her several paces until she came to a stop. I must have looked bereft, because she suddenly said, as if on impulse, Why don't you come to dinner one night? I'll invite my brother, you can see our funny little family in action. Do you have any siblings?

No, I said.

She nodded, as if she now understood something about me. I've often wondered what it would be like, she said, to not have a brother or a sister. Or rather, I have been thinking about it a great deal, of late. Abruptly, she turned to go. I will email you, she called over her shoulder, we'll find a day. Before I could reply, she had hurried off. As I watched her go, I felt my phone vibrating in my bag. I immediately retrieved it, heart racing. The screen was black and there were no messages. I must have imagined the vibration. I looked up. Eline had disappeared from sight and I was alone. I stood in the middle of the sidewalk, there was a sharp and unpleasant wind. I counted the days and then I counted them again. It had been over a week since I had asked Adriaan when he was coming back, how things stood with Gaby, it had been another week of silence.

12.

I moved out of Adriaan's apartment that weekend. I could no longer see any reason to stay, there was nothing for me to do except leave. I went through the apartment and I gathered my things—piece by piece by piece I withdrew. There was more of me there than I thought, as I continued to fold my clothes and collect my papers, doubt surged up inside me. And once I had packed my bags and as I stood in the doorway with my suitcases, I felt doubt and also regret. I looked around the apartment where I had spent the past month, and was overcome at the idea of never returning. How had this happened? I was aware even then that I was acting on a feeling that might yet fade or otherwise mutate. But on some level it was too late. I turned to go and realized that I did not know where to leave the keys. The mailbox did not seem sufficiently secure, not when I did not know how long it would be before his return. And so after I had locked the door behind me, I put the keys at the bottom of my bag. I gave myself that.

It was an adjustment, moving back to my old apartment. I was somehow less at home there than I had been in Adriaan's apartment. The place felt as if it belonged to a stranger, or a person I no longer recognized. The temporary nature of the accommodation was more glaring than before, it was as if the rooms had been hollowed out in my absence, as if the walls were now made of paper. Despite myself I was still waiting—for Adriaan to come back, at the very least for him to respond to the message I had sent, asking if we could speak.

I did not tell him that I had moved out of the apartment. Perhaps some part of me thought that if we spoke, if he explained the reasons behind his silence, I might go back to the apartment, unpack my bags as if nothing had happened, wait for his return. But he did not respond and for days the silence from Lisbon occupied me, like a fog in the brain. Eline's email, when it arrived, briefly interrupted the monotony of that waiting. She invited me to dinner the following week. It would be herself and her brother, a small and simple gathering while the boys were with their father and her brother's wife was out of town, she had invited Jana but unfortunately she was busy. Still, she hoped that I would join them. I replied to say that I would come, and that I was looking forward to it.

Her house, when I arrived, was lit throughout. The drapes were drawn back against the darkness, as if to declare that the residents of this home had nothing to hide. I stood outside and wondered what it would be like to live so exposed, to be so fearless. From the street, you could see directly into the ground level, and although there were no figures, the room was like a stage set, there was a great deal of intimate information in the details visible through the drapes, the large kitchen table and the clutter of children's toys, a dog bowl and bed.

As it turned out, those items belonged not to Eline, but to the tenants who occupied the lower apartment. She lived in the top floors with her sons, who were of course too old for the toys I had seen through the window, had I thought even for a moment I would have realized my mistake. I would have realized that the woman I had met at the museum and at the café, the woman whose brother had only recently been assaulted to the point of hospitalization, could not be living in such an innocent way—that woman would lock the doors, close the drapes, switch on the security cameras, that woman was living in a state of considerable fear and anxiety.

But I didn't think, or it didn't occur to me, perhaps because I was at that point still unable or unwilling to reconcile the woman I had met with the situation she was in. Instead, I had in mind the family that occupied the ground-floor apartment, the aura of their happy chaos with me as I rang the doorbell expectantly, it was the kind of life I would have wanted Eline to have, the kind of life I would have wanted to have myself. I therefore experienced a small shock when a man opened the door and I saw beyond him the monochrome interior, cold and perfect, with not a single ornament out of place.

But it was the man himself who was most jarring—it was the brother, Anton de Rijk. And although I had come to this house with the clear understanding that I would be meeting him, I found that I was not prepared, I was still startled by his appearance. How was it that I had failed to imagine the extent of his injuries, how was it that I was surprised by the large and vivid scar across his forehead, still puffy and puckered at the edges? Or the fact that he was breathing heavily as he leaned against the door, as if struggling with a lung that had recently been punctured, a set of bruised and broken ribs? His face was faintly distorted, as if he had suffered nerve damage, some features crumpled, others that veered off. I remembered that he had been hospitalized, for over a week, Jana had said.

He remained there, his body propped against the door, I

was aware that I was staring. He nodded, as if I had con-
firmed something, either about himself or about myself. No
doubt in the wake of the assault he had grown used to people staring. His face was a version of Eline's face in the way
that a photographic negative is a version of the photograph
itself. I thought this would have been the case even before
the assault, he had none of her beauty, on some level his
features simply registered as a coarsened version of hers.
And yet they had a quality that was in some way primal, as
if his was the originating mold. If it was lacking in beauty
his face nonetheless had some dark charisma, it was memo-
rable in a way that Eline's was not. As I stood before him, I
could feel myself forgetting what Eline looked like, I began
only to recollect her face as a distant echo of his.

With some visible effort he at last pushed himself upright and stepped aside, bidding me enter. You're Eline's
friend, he said, and I nodded and said hello. He turned and
I saw that he moved with the aid of a cane, an ornate and
lacquered instrument that was old-fashioned, entirely unlike the rubber and aluminum braces that are more common now. The effect was to make his injuries seem more
inherent to his character, less temporary and more integral.
As I followed him through the well-appointed foyer with
its large mirrors and neutral hues, I saw that he was walking
with a marked limp, dragging one leg heavily behind him.
He wore expensive dress shoes, polished to a meticulous

gleam, I wondered if he did that himself or if someone else did, a butler or a manservant, a figure as anachronistic as his cane. The sole on the side that dragged was thicker, the shoe had been outfitted with a lift, and I thought then that the limp must have been part of a long-standing condition, pre-dating the attack.

I followed him until we at last reached a large and airy kitchen, where Eline stood at the counter. She looked up and made a sound of annoyance, You should have told me, I didn't hear the bell, she said. She smiled apologetically at me, as her brother made his way to the kitchen table. He sat down, leaning back into his chair and gazing at her. I watched in fascination as he pushed his tongue out of his mouth, so that it lolled against his lips, a gesture that was at once obscene and playful. She made a sound of quiet exasperation and then turned to me. Welcome, she said. You met my brother, Anton.

Yes, I said, although he had not in fact introduced himself. I thought it was surprising that Eline had not opened the door herself, she did not exactly fuss over her brother (no doubt he was the type of man who would have batted away such ministrations), but she treated him with visible concern. He reached for the bottle of wine that sat on the table, I saw that it was already near empty. Eline resumed chopping some herbs, she glanced at him several times before she abruptly asked, Are you supposed to be drinking

on those painkillers? I thought the doctor said not. He ignored her, I was still standing in the middle of the kitchen,
perhaps it was not too late to quietly back out of the room
and leave the house unnoticed.

Sit down, Anton suddenly said to me, as if he had intuited the thought. He gestured with his wineglass to the
chair beside him. I would rather have joined Eline behind
the counter, but he was not a man whose injunctions were
easily ignored. I sat down obediently. He exchanged glances
with Eline, then reached for an empty glass and poured me
some wine.

Anton is in a bad mood, Eline said. She said this in a
manner that was entirely matter-of-fact, as if it were neither unusual nor particularly serious. A deal gone bad? she
asked. She was no longer really paying attention, she had
turned back to the stove. He shrugged and watched me as
he sipped from his glass. Just trying to clean up the mess
made in my absence, he said. That idiot Vincent let go of
some good firsts for next to nothing, and the inventory's in
total disarray. I work in books, he added to me, by way of
explanation. Anton has a beautiful shop in the Old Town,
Eline said.

Yes, I said automatically, I've been there. I felt Anton's
eyes slide toward me. Did you buy anything? he asked casually. Yes, I said. In fact I spent more than I intended. I
was looking for a gift for someone. I laughed, too loud and

nervously. He nodded. Most of the sales are online, of course, he said. But the storefront is more important than you might think. Just the other day, a man walked in and asked for forty meters.

Eline looked up. Forty meters of what?

Leather and gilt, he said. Old-fashioned. Classic.

Ah, she said. An interior designer.

He could only speak in the language of his mood board, it was really quite extraordinary. Tobacco. Royal blue. Plush. Traditional. I asked him if he was interested in a particular author, or a particular genre. But no. These books aren't for reading, he explained. They're for—creating a look, an atmosphere. Anton waved a hand before his face as if to evoke a delicate perfume. He dropped his hand. Of course, we were happy to oblige. Forty meters of books is a great many books, tens of thousands of euros' worth of books. And he truly didn't care in the least what was inside them, a kind of Jay Gatsby if you see what I mean.

Goodness, murmured Eline, I could see that she had lost interest in the story.

But that's not all, he added hurriedly. That's not the end. She looked up, he had her attention again. We sold him a lot of worthless junk, subscription editions, encyclopedias, remaindered monographs, that kind of thing—the prices only very slightly inflated, of course. He grinned, so that we knew the opposite was true, and I saw Eline glance at me, perturbed. And the point is, she murmured.

The point is, the point is—you're always hastening toward the denouement, Eline, he said irritably. It's very tedious of you.

Yes, I know, she said, her hands resting on the countertop. She looked at me with a smile. Anton loves to tell stories. He loves—digressions. He takes longer to tell a story than anyone I know. Although it's true the digressions generally do have a point, at least eventually. She paused and looked back at her twin. Go on, then.

He gave an elaborate sigh and leaned forward, propping his hands on his cane. It was clear now that the cane and the limp were not the result of the assault, but something he had been born with or lived with for some time. In that light, his flamboyance seemed different, a manifestation of his vulnerability, and also his resilience. I felt ashamed of the assumptions I had made about this man, with his expensive shoes and his pressed shirts, I remembered how fondly Eline had spoken of him, it was more than familial loyalty, her twin had saved her during the breakup of her marriage, he had been an uncle and a father to her sons.

He continued to address Eline, but his gaze was on me, his body turned in my direction, as if he had detected the shift in my sympathy. Last week, I went to Lars and

Lotte's new house for the first time. Of course, they bought the house nearly a year ago, but we generally meet in restaurants or bars, Lotte doesn't like to cook. But this time, they invited me to the house, given the circumstances, they thought I would be more comfortable there.

There was a hard edge to his voice, and Eline frowned and then said, But they were right, Anton. It is far more comfortable for you to be there.

I don't mind people staring.

It's not a question of people staring. Anyway, I always prefer to eat at someone's home, that's why—and she looked at me apologetically—we're here tonight.

Let me finish my story.

Of course.

I was very conscious of the fact that I was being invited to their new home for the first time. Miriam was away so I limped—it was the first time he had referred to his physical impediments, from the corner of my eye I thought I saw Eline flinch—over to the fancy deli and bought a bottle of wine and some chocolates, I don't know, usually it's Miriam who handles these things, but as I've said, she was away.

Eline was looking at him with an expression that was troubled, and I wondered where Miriam was now.

So I arrive, with my chocolates and my bottle of wine, neither of which seems entirely right. Even from the outside the house is tremendous. Enormous, a nineteenth-century townhouse but with glass cubes affixed to the façade in random places, almost likes postmodern growths. Inside, the house is even more impressive, it's one of those new smart houses, with solar panels and a self-watering green roof to regulate the temperature, an atrium through the middle of the house, everything synced up to an iPad, I have no idea how they got the permits to do such things.

Eline was bringing bowls of soup to the table. Anton barely paused as he picked up his spoon, took a mouthful of soup, and reached for some bread. She set her own bowl down and sat across the table from him. She looked at me. Cheers, she said drily. He nodded in acknowledgment of the food, eating with extraordinary gusto and speed, and then continued.

I thought, I knew they were doing well, but I didn't realize they were doing *this* well. And I wasn't surprised they hadn't invited anyone over yet, Lotte nervously explained that the house wasn't finished, she said they would have a housewarming party as soon as they had fully moved in, and then suddenly added something about buying the house because it had such a good space for entertaining, they would be able to host fund-raisers and charity events. I nodded, they were clearly embarrassed by the incontrovertible evidence of their wealth, which had crossed over from the

merely excessive to the truly obscene, without any of us
really noticing.

But we all knew they were doing well, Eline said. She
turned to me. Lars is a property developer, he's responsible
for those new apartments around the old train station. I
nodded, those buildings had contributed to the rise of prices
in Jana's neighborhood and represented some of the fiercest
gentrification in the city. I thought that Lars would have
been a controversial figure in some circles, and I wondered
if this was why he had kept so quiet about the expansion of
his considerable fortune. Eline had used the word *responsible*, although that didn't necessarily imply any particular
judgment on her part, she had spoken neutrally enough.

Yes, Anton said. I knew they were doing well. He turned
to address me and said by way of explanation, The money is
from Lotte, who is as stupid and bourgeois as her name. But
Lars is different, he's a cunning animal and he's turned all
that nice old money into a real fortune. He laughed. You
know, those buildings he's put up are a total monstrosity,
from an aesthetic point of view as well as a moral one.

I haven't seen them, Eline said.

Haven't you? Anton asked.

She looked away. Jana had first met Eline close to the
site of the assault, if she had ventured so far into the neighborhood she would have seen the buildings, at least periph-

erally. I thought it likely Anton did not know that she had made the trip to the neighborhood, and I wondered what else she had not told him, what other secrets there might be between them.

Anyway, Anton continued, this house, it was a far cry from the monstrosities he's built his fortune on, when it's a question of his own living environment, he knows how to feather his nest. I thought it was a strange phrase, old-fashioned and a little affected, in the manner of his cane. He pressed on. Despite a certain initial coyness in their manner, I quickly realized that they were actually quite excited to be showing off their home, they dragged me from room to room, showing me the vast expanses of marble, the custom light fittings, the restored tile on the fireplace, I assure you once they hit their stride they were perfectly sanguine about hauling a cripple up and down the stairs.

Anton, Eline said in protest.

Well, I am, he said. With me, Lars and Lotte can wallow in their privilege without shame, Lotte can talk about the wallpaper and the finishes, it doesn't matter how idiotic she appears because she's only doing it before me, the cripple. I'm not exactly subhuman, but we all know where we stand in the pecking order, I'm several notches lower than the likes of them. Particularly in my current condition, such things simply don't happen to people like Lars and Lotte.

But it might just as easily have—

Never mind, Anton said. Never mind, that isn't the point. Let me finish. So Lars and Lotte are dragging me all over the house, the kitchen, the pantry, the guest room, even into their bedroom for Christ's sake, with the king-sized bed and the Frette linens and the foul stench of bourgeois sex, which is of course the most perverse sex of all, when Lotte opens a final door and says in a voice of particularly shy triumph—oh, I do like Lotte, it's not her fault she's so stupid—And this is the library.

Oh no.

I blinked. Anton gave Eline something of a stern look and then turned back to me and hurried on.

She ushered me into the room, it's impossible to know if she was truly proud of the room or if she simply imagined I would like the room because of my profession. But in any case I was truly gobsmacked, my jaw dropped open, before me were the meters and meters of books that had been re-quested by that idiotic interior designer, the encyclopedias and the remaindered monographs, the whole moronic col-lection that we had sold to that fool at triple, quadruple, quintuple the value, neatly arranged on the built-in shelves. I started laughing, I stood in the middle of the library and I laughed and laughed and after a moment Lotte became quite worried, and asked whatever on earth was the matter. I recovered enough self-control to assure her that it was only that I was overwhelmed with delight, never in my life had I been in such a beautiful library. She wasn't immediately convinced, I'm known for a certain amount of irony, I could see she was wondering if I was making fun of her.

That's horrible.

Don't worry, I did convince her in the end. We came downstairs—Lars had gone back into the kitchen some time ago, to check on the food—and she positively trilled out to Lars, Anton loves the library, he said it's the most perfect library he's ever seen in his life. Lars looked at me, I could see in his face that he knew—not that I'd sold him the books, Lars would not have been the one to deal with the interior designer—but he knew that I'd been mocking Lotte. The rest of the dinner, he couldn't even bring himself to look in my direction, he had nothing but contempt for me. But Lotte was in excellent humor, and I saw him give her a look of such—such tenderness, such deep affection and love.

He had slowed at last, and now he looked up at Eline. They do love each other, you know. Despite all the money. Lars would kill for Lotte, I'm sure of it. Kill me, if it came down to it.

Eline shook her head and rose to her feet. Are you done? she asked with a smile. I nodded, and she began clearing the table. At any rate, she said to Anton, you don't come off very well in that story.

I never think about coming off well in a story, he said calmly. You have to give me that.

Eline returned with a platter of fish and cold boiled potatoes and then refilled our wineglasses. Still, she said with a sigh as she looked down at Anton. Cheers. I'm grateful that you're here. Anton was in a very bad accident, she said to me, it's been a difficult couple of months. It happened close to where Jana lives.

Jana? Anton asked.

Our mutual friend, I said. I waited for Eline to say more, about the manner of her meeting with Jana, but she remained silent and began serving the food.

Eline is putting a spin on the matter, Anton said as he handed his plate to his sister. I was attacked. There was nothing accidental about it. Accident sounds more humane, normal people are in accidents but only idiots and the unlucky are attacked. I looked at Eline, her face was drawn, she looked pained and irritated, though not, I noted, especially embarrassed. She handed Anton back his plate. I was mugged, Anton continued as he took the plate. Mugged and assaulted. It's the neighborhood, you know.

I'm sorry, I said. I wondered—

About the scar? And the bruises? Yes, that's all from the attack, they took my phone and my wallet and my watch, but they also beat me very brutally. He paused. The malice is what's frightening. They didn't need to do it, they had my money. I wasn't exactly resisting.

Was it more than one person?

He shook his head. I can't remember, he said.

How did your meeting with the police go? Eline asked.

Anton cut into his food. Chewing, he lowered his fork and knife to his plate. He took a sip of wine and then swallowed. They had me do a session with a hypnotist, he said at last.

A hypnotist? Eline asked, startled.

Yes.

I had no idea they did such things. Did it work?

He leaned back into his seat. Well, I was myself quite surprised. I arrived at the station, they had asked me to come in for some follow-up questions. I was taken into an office, given a coffee, that sort of thing. And then they told me that they wanted to try something a little unorthodox— if I was willing, of course. He paused. I said that I was willing and I asked what they had in mind.

What did he look like?

Who?

The hypnotist.

Anton shrugged. He was dressed like a low-level bureaucrat. I thought he was another detective at first. He did have a very soothing voice, however. I was of course wary,

I don't go in for that sort of thing, I don't believe in it. But I agreed. I'd never been hypnotized before and there was something rather compelling about the man, I have to admit.

And did it work? Eline leaned across the table, her face intent.

No.

Nothing new?

I'm afraid not. He did the whole rigmarole, taking me back to the moment of the attack, putting me in my body or was it taking me out of my body? Either way, it was of no use whatsoever. I can't remember a damn thing, whether or not I'm hypnotized. I only know what I was told after the fact.

He reached for his wineglass again. He took a long drink, his eyes blinking restlessly. Eline cleared her throat, It's a kind of amnesia, she explained to me. He can't remember anything about the night of the assault.

It's apparently very common after a severe concussion, Anton said. Obviously, this is endlessly frustrating to the police. They keep hoping I'll remember something and as you can see, have resorted to desperate measures.

You don't remember who attacked you? I asked.

No. I don't remember anything—who attacked me, or why I was in that neighborhood, which I'm not exactly in the habit of frequenting, I've never been there before in my life, it's a real shithole, not the kind of place I'm likely to go. Apologies to your friend. He looked down, his eyes shifting and his mouth tense, I had the definite feeling that he was lying. I suppose it's a sort of selective amnesia, he continued, his voice silky and too smooth. The brain's response to the awful trauma of the whole thing.

What I don't understand, Eline said, is the fact that you can't remember why you were there. I can understand why you can't remember the assault itself, why there might be amnesia around the concussive event—I could see that she was struggling with the language, and I wondered if perhaps she didn't believe him either, it wasn't just me, there was something unconvincing about the entire matter. But the reason why you went there in the first place, that would have been something you would have known from the period before the trauma, presumably.

How should I know? he said roughly. If I knew, I wouldn't be in this predicament. It's not exactly pleasant you know, it's not as if I'm doing it on purpose. My body was already a ruin, and now my mind is as well. His voice had grown petulant and his face flushed. It's as if a piece of my brain has been removed and no amount of trying will bring it back. The police think if only they ask the right question the key will turn and the floodgates will open and I'll be able to pick out the perpetrators from a convenient police lineup. But it doesn't happen. I've sat there for hours. I've looked at my diary, at my messages. I let myself be hypnotized for Christ's sake. But there's nothing.

Shh, Eline said, and she reached her hand out to him. Calm down. He shook her hand off. Yes, he said viciously, that's what Miriam says as well.

A silence fell upon the table. He knows, I suddenly thought. He knows more than he is saying. Eline began clearing the table and I got up to help her. There was fruit for dessert, and shortly after I said that I should be going, the Court was in session the following day and I would need to get a good night's rest. The shadow of loneliness had crept upon me as I watched Eline and her brother, for all their bickering and all the secrets between them, they shared an air of intimate collusion, of things implied and understood. Anton nodded, to my surprise he also rose to his feet, saying that he too would be going. He followed me down the corridor. I was aware of his presence in a new way, as we both pulled on our coats, and when I turned to say thank you to Eline I saw a startled look of warning in her eyes.

Outside, Anton walked with me half a block until I saw a taxi and I said that I thought I should take it. He flagged the car and opened the door for me in a courtly fashion, as I got in I said that it had been very nice meeting him. He leaned forward and said that he hoped that he would see me very soon. His voice was mischievous and there was something lewd in the movement of his body toward mine, so that I was suddenly made nervous. Still, it occurred to me that it might not be safe for Anton to walk the streets alone, not in his condition, and after a moment I asked if he wanted a ride. I was aware this might have sounded like an invitation of sorts, although that was not my intention. However, he was already walking away, he shook his head and waggled his cane through the air. Not tonight, he called back over his shoulder, not tonight.

13.

I sent Eline an email thanking her for dinner. She wrote back to say that she was glad I had made it home okay, a statement that seemed at least in part to refer to her brother, and to which I wasn't entirely sure how to respond. It occurred to me that she was fishing for information, which made me even more uncertain, and for that reason her email languished in my in-box, unanswered.

The following week, Amina went on maternity leave. Robert was now my regular partner in the booth and we quickly grew accustomed to each other. He was kind, and seemed to understand that these new circumstances would require an adjustment on my part. At the end of our first day working together he accompanied me down to the lobby and warned me to pace myself. The trial will last for many more months. You have to think of it as a marathon. We had reached the entrance and he paused to help me pull on my coat. Months, I said, as I fastened the buttons and tied a scarf around my neck. I could hear the disbelief in my voice, although I already knew how long the trial could last. He patted me on the shoulder. Not to sound patronizing, he said, but you will get used to it. It becomes normal.

He was right. As soon as the following week, I noticed that the extremity of the trial—its content and language, the physical demands of being in the booth—had started to recede. I was less depleted at the end of each day, despite the fact that by this point in the trial we were mired in technicalities, the sessions dragged on for hours of testimony that were mind-numbingly precise and rarely resolved into an obvious advantage for either the prosecution or the defense.

I also came to understand, over the course of those sessions in the courtroom, how disciplined the former president really was. The polo neck and chinos were replaced by the tailored suit and with it came a somber, even dignified, mien. I understood then the tremendous will that powered the man. Unlike the lawyers and on occasion judges, his face never betrayed him. Instead, he wore the same expression throughout the proceedings, one of keen but impersonal interest. He maintained the affect of a star debater on a university team, somebody who was looking for openings, who took note of everything, a man who conceded nothing and had nothing to conceal. Not once did I see the sullen indifference that I had observed on the faces of other men on trial, that I had seen on his own face in the conference room, an expression that seemed to declare that whatever was taking place was of little interest, and guilt a foregone conclusion.

No, he was nothing like the man I saw in the conference room—although perhaps I had always known that this person, this polished and ruthless competitor, lurked inside the more impulsive character I encountered in those meetings. During this period, he did not take the stand, and yet each gesture he made was highly calculated. Upon entering the courtroom, he would look up at the public gallery, at his audience, and nod in acknowledgment of his supporters, of which there were still many, so many that I wondered whether they had traveled to The Hague to be there, and how they could afford the money and the time to stay in the city for weeks on end, what kind of life they were living in this rainy place.

Then his gaze would travel across the gallery, over to the interpreters' booths, where I was sitting. He would look directly at me, through the glass window, and nod. As if to recognize the work that I performed, as if to demonstrate the level of his civility and consideration. This became routine, but the first time it happened it was so unexpected that it felt unreal, as if he had ruptured some fourth wall. Robert made a small, startled movement and I felt myself growing hot. Down in the courtroom, Kees craned his neck to look up at the booths. I hesitated and then nodded awkwardly in return, I didn't know what the etiquette was in such matters. The former president then began speaking to a junior member of his defense counsel. Still seated, I looked over and saw that some of the supporters in the public gallery were now looking curiously in my direction, the gesture had not gone unnoticed. On the courtroom floor, Kees returned to his papers, slowly shaking his head.

From then on, the former president never failed to acknowledge me, both at the start of each session and then again at the end. In those first days in Chamber I, I was certain that I would never grow accustomed to this moment of recognition, the meaning of which remained unclear to me. Was it mere politesse or was it something more sinister, more calculating and exploitative? But then as Robert had told me, it became normal. We would nod to each other and then we would look away and carry on.

Over the course of those long hours in the booth, I sometimes had the unpleasant sensation that of all the people in the room below, of all the people in the city itself, the former president was the person I knew best. In those moments, out of what I can only describe as an excess of imagination, he became the person whose perspective I occupied. I flinched when the proceedings seemed to go against him, I felt quiet relief when they moved in his direction. It was disquieting in the extreme, like being placed inside a body I had no desire to occupy. I was repulsed, to find myself so permeable. With increasing frequency, I avoided looking down into the courtroom, I concentrated on the notes on the page before me, on the words being spoken into my earpiece. And yet he was always there, sitting to one side of the courtroom, unavoidable and inescapable.

But then the prosecution called to the stand the first of several victims whose testimony, the lead prosecutor promised, would remind the Court of the gravity of the crimes committed by the accused, the moral weight of the issues currently under consideration. Robert had already warned me that the victims' testimony was almost always the most difficult to interpret, he confessed that earlier that year he had been obliged to excuse himself from the testimony of a young mother whose children had been brutally murdered, literally torn from her arms and slaughtered. I have nieces and nephews, he said, his voice shaking, I felt no compunction whatsoever about saying that I couldn't do it.

When I arrived in the booth, Robert was already there. I couldn't tell if he was more subdued than usual, or if it was merely the projection of my own tension, I had never before worked a victim's testimony. He nodded to the booth across from us and I raised my hand in greeting to the visiting interpreters, who raised their hands in return; the witness would be speaking Dyula, which the pair in the opposite booth would interpret into French, and which we in turn would interpret into English. I sat down, I saw that they had drawn the curtains on the windows of the public gallery. Facial distortion software would be used on the video link, the voice would also be altered, utmost caution would be taken so that the witness's identity would not be publicly revealed. Almost all the victims would have family back home, they were taking considerable risk in choosing to appear, risk that might even and without warning be converted into concrete sacrifice, violence or death to their loved ones.

The moral weight of the situation was therefore already evident in the courtroom, and as people began to enter, I thought their expressions were also more than usually somber. There were no smiles, no visible demonstrations of humor, nor was there the frenetic urgency that had sometimes earlier been apparent. Instead, there was a kind of muffled seriousness, one that was not even particularly self-conscious; for once, nobody seemed to be performing, either for themselves or for the benefit of others. Even Kees, when he came in, running his hands through his hair, appeared restrained, he merely sat down and began reviewing the text on the monitor before him.

When the former president was brought into the court-room, I saw at once that he had no intention of submitting to the prevailing mood, that he perceived such tamping down of emotion as a concession to the magnitude of the victim's loss, and thus the severity of the crimes he stood accused of having committed. Or perhaps it was simply that he was unaccustomed to the room's attention being fo-cused elsewhere. I observed the defiance that seemed to roll off him in waves, as he lifted his chin and surveyed the courtroom, his gaze resting without hesitation on the wit-ness stand before moving smoothly on, as if to show he had nothing to fear, no cause for trepidation. I felt a jolt of dis-gust so strong I could taste it in my mouth.

The judges entered. Within moments, or so it seemed to me, the presiding judge had asked for the witness to be brought in. The side door opened and a slender young woman entered. She was obliged to walk past the former president as she made her approach to the witness stand, and did so stiffly and without looking in his direction. He leaned forward, folding his hands on the desk and watching her carefully. She looked no older than twenty. The court usher poured her a glass of water, adjusted the microphone. The witness barely seemed to respond, her face was empty of expression. It was obvious the entire thing was an ordeal for her, she sat rigid in her chair and stared straight ahead, as if afraid to move.

Thank you for joining us today, the presiding judge said. It seemed to me that her voice was softer than usual, as though wary of startling the witness. You have a card on the table with the oath. If you could please read this out.

The young woman wet her lips, then leaned forward and spoke into the microphone. As she spoke, I saw that I had misapprehended her character, what I had interpreted as nerves was instead the extremity of her focus, she had come here to perform a monumental task and it followed that she was a person of no small courage. Her voice, as she read the oath of the Court and swore to speak the truth, was low and strong and supple and it sent a ripple through the room. I saw that I was not alone in recalibrating my sense of this young woman, the former president himself looked up at the sound of her voice and for the first time I saw something akin to fear in his eyes.

The presiding judge was exceedingly solicitous, asking the witness how she was feeling, thanking her for appearing before the Court, and assuring her of the value of her testimony. The young woman nodded, but even as the judge extended to her the sympathies of the Court I could see that she had little use for it, she understood all too clearly its limitations, she had not come all this way for the Court's sympathy but for its promise of justice. The Court already had the witness's statement in the record, the judge said, detailing how her brothers and her father had been killed. She would now be made available for examination by both parties. The judge paused and then said that she was very sorry to be asking her to revisit the events of that terrible day, events that she knew were profoundly upsetting. The trial by its nature demands more from the victims than it does from the accused, the judge said, which is in and of itself another injustice, and for which I can only express my profound regret. The young woman nodded. The judge then said that she would give the floor to the prosecution.

The prosecutor rose to his feet. He said he would be asking the witness questions about one particular day, during the unrest following the election. He would be obliged to ask her to go into considerable detail, for which he apologized. And he also apologized for speaking to her in French, unfortunately he did not speak her language. After a brief pause, during which his words were interpreted, I looked to the booth across the way. The young woman gave a curt nod and the prosecutor cleared his throat and examined his notes before commencing.

You were at home on the day in question, were you not?

The young woman leaned forward and responded.

Yes, I was at home with my family.

But you went out in the morning.

Yes. I went out in the morning with my brothers. It

seemed that things had quieted down, and we wanted to go to the school. There had been gunshots the previous night, coming from that direction.

Her voice remained low and firm. She spoke with great deliberation, so that each word was like a link in a chain and the entire thing held fast, even as it moved across languages. From her to the visiting interpreters to us. The prosecutor nodded.

How far is the school from your home?

Perhaps ten minutes.

And what did you find when you arrived at the school?

The young woman paused and took a sip of water from her glass.

Please take your time.

Her gaze snapped up to the prosecutor. She shook her head, as if to say that she required no special dispensation, and continued.

There were bodies everywhere.

How many?

Thirty-two.

How do you know?

Because I counted.

Why?

What else should I have done?

Her manner was very simple as she said this, and there

was not a drop of self-pity in it. Robert was interpreting and I heard his voice run dry. He continued.

And they were of the targeted ethnicity?

Yes.

How do you know this?

Because they were my neighbors. I grew up with these boys. I knew them very well. I knew their mothers and their sisters. I knew what they liked to eat for their dinner, what they wanted to be when they grew up.

Robert motioned to me and I nodded and took over.

And what happened next?

There were more gunshots. We heard more gunshots, and so we went home as quickly as we could. We ran home.

What happened when you arrived?

Our father pulled us inside and he and my brothers barred the door. We could hear the shouts coming from down the road. I ran outside and hid in the shed.

Where were your father and brothers?

They stayed in the house. I ran out alone.

And what happened next?

As I worked, I was obliged to focus on the voice of the interpreter in the opposite booth, which was measured and precise and occluded much of the sound of the young woman's speech. And yet her voice came through with remarkable clarity in the gaps between interpretation, the syllables distinct, the timbre unmistakable, so that I still had the sense that I was speaking for her, despite the layers of language between us.

I said: There was the sound of shouting coming louder and louder and then the men started banging on the door. I could hear them from the shed outside, I could hear everything. They broke the door down and then they ordered my father and my brothers to lie on the ground. I heard the sound of gunshots and I ran out of the shed and into the house—

Why did you do this?

I paused. Because I wanted to protect my family.

How did you hope to protect your family?

With my body. It is small and it does not look like much but it can stop a bullet.

But you were not able to protect your family?

No. I paused. When I arrived, my brothers were dead. They lay in a line on the floor, facedown. My father was lying on the floor beside my brothers and I begged them not to kill my father, I ran forward so that I could stop them. But one of the men hit me in the head with the butt of his gun and I fell back to the floor and I could not move. I watched as they shot my father in the head. The blood from his wound flowed into the blood of my brothers and I screamed and screamed. They ignored me as they went through the house taking our money and our radio and whatever else they could find, they even ate our food, the food that had been prepared for lunch. They had no respect for the living or the dead, they were laughing as I screamed. As I shook my brothers and I shook my father and I tried to bring them back to life.

I stared across at the booth, and the interpreter looked up as he spoke and as I continued to interpret, and for a long moment we simply stared at each other.

The other interpreter looked down again as the witness paused. Sorry, I did not stop to allow for the interpretation, he said. I apologize. The witness looked up to the booths. I apologize, I said. May I continue?

Someone must have indicated that sufficient time had lapsed because she began once more. As I looked down at the witness, it prickled through me, the strangeness of speaking her words for her, the wrongness of using this *I* that was hers and not mine, this word that was not sufficiently capacious.

I said: And then they left. They did not think me worth killing. I was nothing to them. My grief was nothing to them. They thought of me as entirely insignificant, a little girl, not even worth the bullet it would take to kill me.

The prosecutor nodded. His voice, when he spoke, was very gentle.

And was it your understanding that these men belonged to groups mobilized by the former president in the wake of the election?

Kees rose at once, Your Honor, the witness cannot be expected to make a judgment—

The witness interrupted and he fell silent. My breath caught as I watched her lean forward and speak into the microphone, her arms folded on the desk, her voice steady.

There was a slight delay and then the interpreter in the other booth said, and then I said, the tremble audible in my voice, unlike the voice of the other interpreter, unlike the voice of the witness herself, which remained steady and solid and strong: Yes. There is no doubt in my mind. I know exactly who these men were, and why they were there to kill us. I know exactly who ordered them to exterminate us all.

And as I spoke, I could not help it, my gaze went from the young woman to the former president. Who had no need for these layers of interpretation. Who sat bolt upright and did not move, and whose gaze was trained with utmost attention and care upon the witness.

14.

One week later, I saw Anton in a restaurant close to the Court. I had been taken out for lunch by Bettina. She did not usually socialize with her staff and I knew there had to be something she wished to discuss—likely my contract, and the question of whether I would or would not remain at the Court.

It was something that had begun to weigh upon me, more heavily by the day. Ever since the witness testimony, my time in the booth had become more difficult, and I had started to look at my colleagues differently. They no longer seemed like the well-adjusted individuals I had met upon my arrival, instead they were marked by alarming fissures, levels of dissociation that I did not think could be sustainable. And then there was the question of Adriaan, to which I had no real response. I did not know whether I wished to stay or not. But where would I go, if I were to leave? I was not yet able to envision an alternative. For this reason alone it was not a matter of small interest to me, whether or not the Court would extend my contract.

However, Bettina did not bring up the topic until the end of the meal, and because of this I spent the lunch in a state of some tension, enjoying my food less than I might have. The restaurant was Italian, an old apothecary that had been recently renovated. We were seated at a table close to the kitchen, from which I could observe the whole of the dining room. The restaurant was a popular venue for dates and special occasions, but as it was the middle of the day the tables were filled with business lunches. The Court was not in session that day, nonetheless I was surprised by Bettina's leisurely manner, she ordered a starter and then a main. I thought once we had ordered she would explain to me the purpose of our excursion but she continued to make small talk, as the food arrived and then as we ate. The restaurant had been busy when we arrived but quickly emptied once the hour pushed past two, no one else was lingering over their meal in this way. Still Bettina did not broach the subject. It was only once the waiter asked if we wished to see the dessert menu and Bettina replied for both of us, only once we had ordered our desserts and coffees that she at last turned to me and said, There's something I would like to discuss.

It was at that precise moment that Anton walked into

the restaurant. He entered the dining room with the host, saying something that made the host laugh loudly, perhaps he was narrating one of his lengthy stories. The place had fallen quiet but now was vibrating with energy as the two men made their way across the empty dining room. They talked and gestured with enthusiasm, the host's affection seemed genuine and I thought Anton must have been a regular. His limp was barely perceptible, he was far more energetic than he had been the previous week at Eline's house and was clearly in better spirits. The host led him to a corner table. He sat down and set his cane to one side, then smoothed the cloth with his hands, the table was a prime one and he seemed pleased with the arrangement. The two men continued to exchange their raucous pleasantries before the host at last handed him the menu and departed. Anton lowered the menu and took out a pair of reading glasses, which he settled on the end of his—I now realized—extraordinarily large nose. How was it I hadn't noticed it before? He picked up his phone and began tapping energetically at the screen before he set it down again. The reason I asked you to lunch, Bettina said, and I turned. She was looking at me peculiarly, she had come to a rather substantial pause. No doubt she was wondering why I was so distracted. The reason I asked you to lunch is because we would like to extend your contract and invite you to assume a permanent position here.

Even from across the room I could hear the phone vibrate.

My gaze lurched back, at his corner table Anton picked up
the phone and stared at the screen impatiently, he was waiting for someone. As I watched, he sighed and pulled his
glasses off, he had placed his cane to one side and now
looked around the room, his eyes narrowed and imperious.
He looked directly at me and I quickly looked away, back to
Bettina. She continued, We've been very impressed with
the work you have done with us this year. It's a period that
has not been without complications, a moment of many
transitions for the Court.

I would need to reply, Bettina was already perplexed by
my behavior. I nodded and then said, Thank you. That
wasn't sufficient, but I didn't know what else to say. I
thought distractedly of Adriaan, it was delusional to think
that the relationship was extant, that he might yet return to
me. I knew this. And yet in the moments I was able to see
around my emotion and my ego, I was forced to acknowledge this undignified truth: that it would only take a call or
other missive for my hope to resurrect itself. If Adriaan sent
me a message now, if he said that he was coming back in a
few days and nothing more, I knew that I would look up
and tell Bettina that I would be delighted to accept, my dis-
comfort with the work notwithstanding.

But as it was, in the absence of such a message, I did not
know what to say to her. I had very little more than the

persistence of my feeling for Adriaan, my unreasonable attachment. Across the room, Anton was no longer looking in my direction, I was fairly certain he had not noticed me. He was frowning as he stared at his phone, he was at the point where his anticipation was threatening to curdle into irritation and resentment, perhaps he was meeting an important client, or someone who was offering to sell a rare volume, I thought there was something covetous in his expectancy. Bettina was silent, and I forced myself to continue. The trial has been an interesting challenge, I said, and she nodded sympathetically. What has happened to that witness, where is she now? I asked.

Bettina looked away. That kind of information isn't widely shared. Of course, I murmured. It's a complicated case, she continued. It may well collapse. But regardless of the outcome of the trial and its consequences for the Court, you should be pleased, you have done well. She paused. I wondered what she meant by *its consequences for the Court*, what precisely those consequences might be. At that moment, a blond woman pushed through my line of sight, passing directly behind Bettina. She was dressed in a bright purple double-breasted skirt suit and her legs were muscular and bare, the shins shiny with depilation. She walked with both eagerness and apprehension, as if she were scaling a slippery incline. I peered down and saw that she was wearing a pair of red-soled high heels, a brand of shoe that was notoriously expensive and near impossible to walk in.

The shoes were sexy, or at least they denoted sex in an explicit way, it might have been that they were primarily shoes to fuck in, the kind of shoes that were given by men to women. To my horror, I saw that the woman was making her way toward Anton's table. She wore an expression of giddy determination, as if she would let nothing stand in her way, not the high-heeled shoes nor the slick surface of the floor. As for Anton, he had risen to his feet in a posture of scrupulous and ecstatic attention, he looked exactly like a large dog being presented with a piece of raw meat. She gave a breathless squeal of excitement and hastened her pace, her heels releasing a sudden clatter of noise.

Bettina was still talking. In any case, we would like it very much if you were to stay. There will be a salary increase, and the Court has resources to help you transition more fully into your life here, at least from an administrative perspective. I turned to look at Bettina. What life here? I thought blankly, and then a moment later, painfully. In the face of my silence, Bettina continued, This is not a case of covering Amina's maternity leave, there is a real position for you, a permanent one. She paused. That is, if you want to take it.

I nodded. May I think about it? She sat back, a little disappointed. Of course, take a week to think about it. Two weeks, even, she said. I thanked her, even as I spoke my gaze slid back in the direction of the corner table. Anton and the blond woman were nestled into their seats. She sat very still, her cleavage on the verge of spilling out onto the table, while around her Anton was a flurry of movement, he seemed incapable of keeping his hands off her, he touched her cheeks, her hands, her hair, his mouth moving constantly as he doused her in the current of his speech. She nodded occasionally, smiling shyly, the poor woman seemed overcome by his attention.

As she sat there, blinking in confusion, I saw that despite the powerful charisma of her body, her face was very plain, the individual features unremarkable. But Anton was right to be delighted by his good luck, she was a carnal prospect of no small worth. He was in a state of extreme excitation, so that it seemed as if he might soon burst, he squeezed her hand with such force that she let out a little squawk. She looked at him with an expression of real adoration, staring into his face as he gripped her hand and, with a wicked grin, lowered it to his lap. As I watched them, I understood that Anton was attractive, a man with no small powers of fascination.

Do you have any questions for me? Anything that might help you reach your decision? I swiveled my head back to Bettina. She looked uncertain, my behavior had unnerved her. She leaned back in her chair and said, Where is your family? I don't think I ever asked. It was true, Bettina had never asked me a single personal question. My mother moved to Singapore a few years ago. My father is dead. I'm sorry, Bettina said, and I shook my head. It was some years ago, and it wasn't a surprise. It was even a relief, he was sick for a long time. She cleared her throat. And is Singapore home? she asked, and I shook my head again. I don't think I've spent more than a couple of weeks there. I moved here from New York.

Yes, Bettina said, many at the Court have similar family histories, a certain rootlessness seems almost to be a precondition for the work. I nodded. Out of the corner of my eye, I saw Anton rise and tug the blond woman unsteadily to her feet. She wobbled and I wondered if she was already drunk, Anton had ordered champagne and they had both rapidly emptied their glasses. They made their way across the dining room, he was using his cane and she was trailing a little way after him, her heels clattering on the floor. Probably they were going outside to smoke a cigarette. I turned back to Bettina, I said that I would let her know as soon as I was able, I wouldn't keep her waiting. She nodded, and then I asked her how long she had lived in the Netherlands.

A decade.

It was a long time and yet it was shorter than I thought. She sat in the chair across from me, and she seemed so thoroughly of this city, she understood the language and the customs, the unspoken ideologies of its culture. In the end, it took only a decade to become of a place, and that was not so very long.

There were adjustments, she added as the waiter set down our dessert plates. She waited until he left, and then picked up her fork. It's not a very affordable city, and there is something small scale in the landscape, at least compared to where I am from. I go home when I can. I need to be in the place where I grew up, and Germany is only a short drive away. But I like the Dutch, they are quite neutral as a people, although even that is in and of itself something to adjust to.

At that moment, Anton and the blonde came staggering back into the dining room. He had one arm around her waist and she was leaning heavily into him, with no regard whatsoever for his physical condition. He bore her weight without complaint, his posture more erect than I had ever seen it. The blonde lowered her head demurely onto his shoulder and I saw that the skin at the back of her neck was flushed, her hair disheveled. As they passed, she reached down to adjust her skirt.

I looked away, face hot. There was something grotesque and titillating about the entire scene, they must have gone to the bathroom for a quick fuck, propped against the wall of the bathroom. Or perhaps she had been kneeling on the floor blowing him as he leaned on the wall for support, perhaps she had been propped on the sink, her ass cradled in the basin. They looked, as they settled back into their chairs, smug and a little flushed, and also a little less interested in each other. The waiter soon arrived with their starters, and I thought I saw Anton exhale as he contemplated the plate before him. They had not even begun, they had their entire meal to get through before they could reasonably leave.

The blond woman picked up her fork half-heartedly and sighed. Anton squeezed her hand, as if in commiseration. They were speaking in low tones and in Dutch, and I had no special desire to eavesdrop. And yet my ear seized upon fragments of their conversation, *he's back tomorrow* and *it's a nice place* and then *better than Sampurna*. The word *Sampurna* was familiar and I realized it was the name of a restaurant not far from Jana's apartment, I had passed it several times and noted the sign without ever stopping to go in. I turned sharply to look at them. Anton was busy forking food into his mouth and the blonde was eating quickly. *Relax*, he said and even from across the restaurant I could hear the irritation in his voice. *Nobody knows you here.* I looked down instinctively, as if to hide my face. This woman was undoubtedly the reason Anton had been in Jana's neighborhood, even perhaps the reason for his improbable reticence about the assault.

I looked back up at their table, at their strange and unlikely pairing. I thought then of Miriam—Anton's wife, who was once again absent, and who was being so carelessly betrayed in the dining room where I now sat. I thought of Eline, of how fondly she had spoken of Miriam, she had said she was like a mother to her children. But as I watched them eat their food—Anton had at last fallen silent, and the only sound from their table was the clink of china and cutlery—I realized it wasn't the infidelity that was troubling me. No, what troubled me was the secrecy around it, these hidden undercurrents that remained undisclosed, even to the people who knew him best. I recalled his obvious unease when Eline asked him again whether he remembered anything about why he had gone to a neighborhood that was not his own, and where he would have no reason to travel, except for the one that was presently seated beside him in this restaurant on the other side of town.

And I suddenly felt a shiver of fear—if Anton could not tell even Eline why he had been there, then wasn't that because of Miriam? Wasn't that because, despite the assaults he himself forced upon it, there was nonetheless something sacrosanct in the idea of his marriage, some illusion he could not bear to break, however divorced it might be from the reality that was in this restaurant now? That was the power of a marriage, and in that moment I thought of myself, of Adriaan and Gaby. Despite having moved out of the apartment, despite knowing better, I had still hoped—that I might yet hear from Adriaan, that he would return from

Lisbon free and unencumbered, that I would move back into the apartment and accept the position at the Court that Bettina had just offered to me.

But I knew at last that I needed to accept what was and had been obvious for a long time now. Adriaan would not be coming back to The Hague without Gaby. Their marriage had returned to life, the contract renewed. It was all exactly as Kees had said. Adriaan had gone to Portugal in order to save the marriage, in order for the children to grow up with both parents together in the same household, in order to win Gaby back. Perhaps he had deceived me from the start, or perhaps he hadn't been aware of his own motivations at the time of his departure, when he had asked me to stay in the apartment and said those things to me. Perhaps it was only upon his arrival in Lisbon and his reunion with Gaby that, surprised by the depth of his own feeling, he had understood that he hadn't meant what he had said to me, the invitation to stay, the keys on the counter, all of it a mistake.

Is something the matter? Bettina asked. I shook my head, even as I realized that I was crying, that there were so many tears my vision had blurred.

15.

It was in this state of mind that I returned to Adriaan's apartment. I wanted to retrieve the book that I had purchased at Anton's shop, or at least that was what I told myself. I knew that it was not a good idea, and I knew that there were reasons other than the book for my return. But the impulse was too powerful to resist and I went early the next morning. I entered using the key that I still carried and that had never left the bottom of my bag. The housekeeper had been there since my departure and the apartment was pristine, what traces I had left behind—a smudge on the mirror, residue in the sink—had been carefully removed. I felt, as I moved through the rooms, transparent, as if the container of my skin had been removed. I sat down in the kitchen and ran my hands across the table. The force of recall was startling, I was reminded not of the weeks I had been here alone, but of the times I had been here with Adriaan, the times he had sat across from me at this table. I felt his presence there in the room with me like a trembling in the body.

I was still sitting at the counter when I heard a key slide into the lock, the sound of the front door pushing open. For a moment I thought it might be Adriaan, but something in the manner of the movement at the door wasn't correct and my brief elation turned almost immediately to concern. My entire body tensed, as if it were a burglar, someone making a forced entry. But in reality it was much worse, it was Adriaan's wife. She came into the living room, wearing a long camel coat and carrying a large leather tote but otherwise empty-handed. She looked as if she were returning to the apartment from a meeting, although I did not think this could be the case given the early hour.

She stopped when she saw me and for a long moment we stared at each other. She appeared exactly as she did in the photograph: improbably beautiful and also highly polished, as if she lived in continual expectation of being observed. By contrast, my hair was unwashed and my face bare of makeup. But even under better circumstances, even under ideal circumstances, I could never have competed with Adriaan's wife. I was newly aware of the stain on my shirt. She frowned as she dropped her bag and shed her coat, as she made her way toward me, I felt as though I had been caught in the act—although precisely what that act was I did not know, I did not even know if Gaby knew who I was, or the nature of my relationship with her husband.

She stopped before me, her face puzzled. Perhaps she was wondering why Adriaan had bothered to involve himself with me, or perhaps she was wondering who on earth I could be. Awkwardly, I rose to my feet and stood before her.

We don't know each other, she said at last. I'm Gaby.

Yes, I said stupidly.

You're Adriaan's friend, she said. You've been looking after the apartment. Her voice was bright and a little hard, from which it was clear that *friend* was a euphemism, and that she understood well enough what I was. She paused and looked around the room. The place looks uninhabited, has everything been okay?

I still hadn't told Adriaan that I had left the apartment. I didn't disabuse her of her logical misapprehension and instead nodded. Her manner was not openly hostile, it was studiously neutral. Have you had a coffee? she abruptly asked. She didn't wait for a reply before she moved past me and to the cabinets, she took out two cups. What would you like? Cappuccino? Americano? I said that I would take an Americano, and she nodded and turned back to the machine. I couldn't help but feel that she occupied the space with quiet aggression, that this preparation of coffee was in some way performative, designed to remind me who the true owner of the apartment was.

But of that there could be no question. She handed me my coffee and I took a sip cautiously, as if the cup might be poisoned. I was not the only one feeling wary, she also regarded me with a certain amount of caution, as if I were an unknown and unformed quantity, someone whose presence in her life might suddenly grow volatile. I saw that the encounter was as complicated for her as it was for me, maybe even more so, and I was both astonished and ashamed that I hadn't the imagination to see it earlier, all those times I had spent speculating about this woman.

Still, it did not make me feel any more warmly toward her, and I saw that this too was mutual. She smiled, her expression at once brittle and dazzling. I apologize for dropping in like this, she said, although she did not sound sorry in the least. Did Adriaan warn you? I shook my head, mouth dry. He can be so bad about administrative matters, she murmured, as if the matter of our relationship, mine and Adriaan's, had simply been a question of organization and management. Or perhaps she had meant for the comment to be conspiratorial, two women discussing the foibles of a shared man. I stood before her, uncertain of what she was trying to tell me.

She turned and went to the sink. Everyone will be coming back in a week, she announced over her shoulder as she poured her coffee down the drain. Adriaan, the children as well. She turned to face me and crossed her arms. It was not clear what she meant by *everyone*, whether that included her, whether that implied a reunion of the family. And you? I asked. I looked her in the face, I had nothing really to lose. She shook her head and looked up at the clock. She picked up her bag. I have a meeting in Rotterdam, she said. And although this was no kind of answer, although the way she had shaken her head was completely ambiguous, I nodded.

She went to the desk in the sitting room and opened a drawer, pushing through papers and notebooks, life roughage I had never before seen or dared go through. She frowned as she gathered a pile of documents together and placed them in her bag before shoving the drawer closed again. She retrieved her coat, which she had thrown carelessly over the back of the sofa, and moved in the direction of the front door. What should I do with the keys? I asked. She turned to look at me. Through all the beauty, I saw a glint of cruelty in her eyes. She looked around the apartment, she gave a little shrug. Keep them, I suppose. It makes no difference to me. And without waiting for a response, she turned and left, the door slamming shut behind her.

I did as she said. I returned the keys to my bag and I left the apartment. As I rode the tram across town, it was as if a boulder had dropped into the middle of my mind. In part it was Gaby, she made it difficult to think, she ate up the air around her, and I wondered how Adriaan had lived with her for so long. But it was not really this, or not only this. It was the fact of Adriaan's return. What was its meaning, and why had I not heard of it directly from him? My mind circled back to Gaby's words, had there been an edge of defeat to her voice when she said *the children as well*, as if that were a battle she had lost, custody of the children? Or was it resignation, over the life she had forsaken in Lisbon, the choice she had made to return?

I stared through the window of the tram, speckled with dust and droplets of water. I was due to meet Eline for lunch, I had not seen her since the dinner with Anton. I thought uneasily of my encounter with him the previous day, and I wondered what obligation I was under to tell Eline of it. But almost as soon as I arrived at the café, almost before we sat down at our table, Eline said, Anton said he ran into you yesterday. Her voice was bright and I saw that she was braced for the worst. She looked at me cautiously, her manner at once solicitous and wary. It dawned on me that she believed her brother had or was in the process of seducing me. As she waited for me to reply, her mouth tightening with apprehension, I saw that she had been in this situation before, she was only trying to judge how bad the fallout might be this time around.

Yes, I said. Although I don't think he saw me, he was somewhat preoccupied. She blinked. I could see her recalibrating her thoughts, the parameters of the situation shifting before her. He was with a woman, I said reluctantly.

Oh, she said.

I don't know the nature of their meeting, I said.

She leaned back and the air seemed suddenly charged with the added distance between us. Are they sleeping together? Her voice was brittle, she seemed almost another person. It doesn't matter, she continued without waiting for a reply. I've often thought it was a woman that brought Anton to that neighborhood. She paused. Was she an escort? Anton likes prostitutes, he's used them before. Her voice was too casual, as if she were speaking of a car or cleaning service, and some part of me recoiled.

No, I said. No. They were—they liked each other.

But what was she like?

I shook my head. I couldn't really describe her.

She stared at me for a long moment, then nodded. Something about this whole thing has been wrong from the start, she said. I don't believe Anton when he says he doesn't remember anything about the assault. I know my brother well and I know when he is lying. But why wouldn't he just tell me? Infidelity isn't especially shocking, and it's not as if I would tell Miriam, it's not as if— She stopped. He should know that he can trust me.

Perhaps he feels embarrassed or ashamed, I said. I recalled his words in the restaurant. *Relax. Nobody knows you here.* Or perhaps the woman is married, I continued, and there are other reasons why he can't involve the police. Perhaps it would expose her in some way.

Eline shook her head, and then gave a short laugh. He has the luck of the devil, Anton. The police haven't a clue. Not a single lead. If he's keeping quiet about something, he'll get away with it. There's no evidence, there's nothing, in all the footage from that day. It's as if the assailant never existed. She paused. He loves Miriam, you know. But it is hard to ask her to keep accepting the terms of his love.

Her voice was ruminative, and I knew that she was speaking to herself rather than me. I wondered to what degree she believed the assault had been invented out of whole cloth, another one of Anton's stories. If so, it was a particularly dangerous one, the police would have looked to the public housing block for suspects, there would have been interrogations and more. Consequences that extended far beyond the confines of Anton's and Eline's lives. Perhaps something in my gaze betrayed my thoughts because she suddenly seemed embarrassed. We didn't know each other well enough for these disclosures to bring us closer together, we had exposed ourselves in the wrong way, at the wrong time.

I had the feeling that I would not see her again. I realized it had been some weeks since I had spoken to Jana. I really was quite alone. Perhaps because of this, as we stood to go I asked, There was really nothing, in all those hours of footage? For a moment she wavered, she seemed to understand what she was saying about her brother. Then she shook her head. Nothing. Not so much as a ghost.

16.

One week later, the trial of the former president was put on hold. The presiding judge ordered the prosecutor to provide a brief, outlining how the testimonies and evidence submitted to the Court supported the charges against the accused. The order represented a sea change within the trial; the defense was succeeding in unforeseen ways. I was called into a final meeting with the former president. Despite the potential collapse of the prosecutor's case, I was still unprepared for the atmosphere of strange excitation in the conference room when I arrived at the Detention Center. The former president, as soon as I entered, looked at me with an expression of triumph, he nodded to the chair beside him and told me to sit down. Only two members of his team were there, the scene had a last-day-of-school feel to it. I reached for a pad and paper, there were a handful of phrases that they wanted to check in the testimony of the last witness, the lawyer explained, would I oblige them.

From the start, the former president made little pretense of following the conversation, and it wasn't long before he exclaimed, But none of this matters, none of this matters any longer. His manner was petulant, as it always was when he was confronted with the articulation of his crimes. The lawyer looked at him from across the table and then asked if he would like to take a break. The former president shrugged, his defense team had done an extraordinary job for him, and yet, even as the possible end of the trial drew near, his contempt for them seemed to grow, he could already see ahead to the time when he would no longer need them.

If you need a break, then of course, the former president said. The lawyer wearily rose to his feet. Would you like anything? he asked me, and I shook my head. He left the room, although the junior associate remained. The former president turned to me. I apologize for my colleague, he said loftily. It has been a long trial, very tiring for all of us. He spoke as if he himself were part of the defense team, I supposed in some respects that was true. The president seemed to notice my unease. An expression of dissatisfaction settled onto his face. Is anything wrong? he asked. I shook my head. But yes, he said, there is something wrong. I turned reluctantly. He was watching me, his expression kindly, even concerned. He studied my face for a long moment, then gave a wry smile.

Ah, he said. I see. You think I am a bad person. Despite the fact that the case against me will—it now seems almost certainly—be thrown out. You know, my lawyers tell me I may be released in a matter of weeks. I will soon be a free man. He paused. And yet these false accusations and false testimonies have poisoned your mind against me. He held up a hand. Don't apologize, he said. Although I wasn't going to. This little theater here at the Court can warp even the clearest minds. I stared straight ahead, body immobile.

You know, he continued after a pause, the first time I saw you I thought: I like this woman, because she is not truly from the West. But in the end, you are part of the institution that you serve. Across the room, the junior associate was very still, his head bent over his papers. The former president exhaled slowly. Even so, you must see that the justice of this Court is far from impartial, you come from a country that has committed terrible crimes and atrocities. Under different circumstances your State Department would be on trial here, not me. Everyone knows this to be the case. As for your race—he paused, his eyes shifting toward me. Well, the less said about that terrible history the better.

I could not stop the sharp intake of breath, the heat that gathered in my skin. There was very little air in the room.

In the corner, the light on the security camera blinked. The former president continued to watch me. He smiled, as if we were simply making conversation. But then his face stiffened, the congeniality and charm withdrew. He leaned back into his chair. You sit there, so smug. As if you are beyond reproach, he said. He turned to look at me, his face mere inches from mine. But you are no better than me. You think my morals are somehow different to those of you and your kind. And yet there is nothing that separates you from me.

He sat up again and made a curt gesture of dismissal. You may go, he said as he adjusted his tie and leaned forward to examine the papers before him. Slowly, I stood up and gathered my things. My legs seemed to drift beneath me and I almost stumbled as I pulled open the door. I was not able to look at the former president as I left the room, I did not say goodbye. As I made my way down the corridor the junior associate came hurrying after me. He called out and I stopped, leaning against the wall. He stood before me, his face bewildered.

Why didn't you say anything? Why did you let him speak that way to you?

Because he didn't say anything that was untrue.

We stood for a long moment. We understood each other and yet we did not agree. The junior associate was a man who believed himself to be objective. He could not imagine his own complicity, it was not in his nature. But I was different. I wasn't one of them, I didn't have it in me. He shook his head and turned to go.

He doesn't even mean it, he said over his shoulder. It's a manipulation. It's what he does.

I know, I said.

I turned to go. I walked away so quickly that I was almost running and then I was running. I collected my bag and I pushed through the doors and emerged out of that darkness and into the cold outside. The cars rushed by me, I heard a horn blare and I jumped back. My hair whipping across my face. I couldn't return to the Court. I walked instead toward the sea, onto the dunes, I walked until I could see the water and the sound of the tide blocked out the road and the city and the Detention Center and the man inside. I stood there for a long time and then I sat in the sand. The sun was dipping down slowly toward the water.

I took out my phone and called my mother in Singapore. It would be late there, but I thought she might still answer. She did after the first ring, we were not in the habit of regularly speaking and I immediately heard the concern in her voice. Is everything okay? In that moment I did not know how to answer and then I told her that I needed to decide whether or not I would stay in The Hague. The wind had picked up and she said, I can't hear you, the line is so bad. Where are you? I'm on the beach, I said, it's the wind.

Oh, she said and her voice seemed to calm. We took you to that beach once. The one in Den Haag?

The dunes, I said. On the edge of the city.

Yes, she said. We took you there one weekend, the weather was terrible. Your father didn't mind though. You ran up and down the dunes with him until you were both worn out and then we ate poffertjes. Do you remember those? Have you been eating them? You loved them when you were little.

I don't remember coming here as a child.

To Den Haag? I suppose you were very young. We traveled a lot in those days. She didn't seem to realize that she was saying anything of significance, perhaps to her it was only a small and mundane fact of family history. Still, her voice was warmed through with nostalgia. The wind was pressing the hair into my face again and I pushed it aside and looked around. I tried to see the landscape clearly, I tried to understand the feeling of recognition that now overcame me. My mother had fallen silent, and now she asked if I was really okay. You seem very far away, she said and her voice sounded suddenly wistful.

I'm fine, I said. I'm okay.

We hung up moments later. But I remained on the beach

and when I rose to my feet the sun had set long ago, and I had been sitting in darkness for some time.

The case against the former president was formally dismissed two weeks later. We had all known it was possible, the prosecutor's brief, once submitted, had been less than convincing. There had been weaknesses to the case from the start, problems in proving chain of command. From a moral perspective, the man was guilty; from a legal perspective, the man was likely innocent. That both those things were possible was of course understood. But it was another thing to see the case fail before us, to see the cracks begin to widen one by one. I saw uncertainty spread through the building, blooming like mold.

Even before the case was dismissed, the apportioning of blame had begun. I viewed this activity from a distance, but I knew that within the various departments it was swift and vicious, and I was not the only one to wonder how long the prosecutor would last. For several days, there were a great many journalists at the Court—in the lobby, the corridors, on certain days they virtually occupied the cafeteria, thrusting chairs in place to form groups as they huddled over their coffee, their manner always urgent and professional. We regarded them with both suspicion and awe, they possessed the ability to direct attention to a particular event, person, or place with the press of a button, and they were now using that power to direct the world's gaze on the Court.

We interpreters were only extras passing behind the central cast and yet we moved with caution, we had the sense of being under observation. We understood that the story of the trial was being written, and also the story of the Court, whose reputation would be deeply affected by the case. The former president had already released a statement denouncing the Court as a tool of Western imperialism and an ineffectual one at that, for obvious reasons he felt vindicated by the collapse of the case against him. Most of the journalists came to the Court only for opening and closing statements. Having been absent for the many months and years of the trial, they had returned to observe the final moments and attendant chaos. They had mere fragments of the narrative, and yet they would assemble those fragments into a story like any other story, a story with the appearance of unity.

One afternoon, I saw that a group of journalists had gathered in a cluster in the lobby. From a distance and over their heads and outstretched devices, I saw Kees, standing at the center. He was gesticulating to the assembled crowd and I saw the conviction with which he relayed his message, everything was calculated, from the way he looked into the camera to the way he made eye contact with the individual journalists, the careful articulation as he brought his thumb and index finger together, then splayed the fingers out in a single sweeping movement of muted, respectful triumph.

He finished his statement and then there was a rush of questions, phones thrust closer to him, journalists calling his name. He leaned forward as he listened to the journalist who had prevailed, and then—as if he had felt my gaze in particular upon him, out of the half a dozen people looking at him, half a dozen or perhaps more—he looked up from the woman who was asking her question, up and across the lobby, to where I stood. The expression on his face was unreadable, but there was no question that he was looking at me. Several journalists turned to see who or what he was looking at. He stared a moment longer and then nodded once—almost certainly in farewell—before lowering his head once more to the journalist.

That same week, I told Bettina that I would not be able to accept her offer to remain at the Court. She did not seem that surprised, perhaps she had been expecting it given the delay in my response, perhaps it didn't matter given the disorder engulfing the Court, or perhaps she had begun to suspect what I already knew, that I was not suited to the work. Still, she asked me in a mild voice if there was any particular reason why I was declining the position. I told her the truth: that I did not think I was right for the job. Her face grew sympathetic, and I tried to elaborate, I told her that in the end I did not think I was truly qualified for the position.

Your qualifications are excellent, she said, her forehead creasing in confusion. And your work has been consistently very strong. We would not have made the offer if there had been any question about your qualifications. She paused. There is also the issue of temperament. Some people do not have the right temperament for the job and perhaps you are one of them. If that is the case, it is better to know sooner than later, for your own sake but also for ours.

I nodded. I saw that she had already started to dismiss me in her mind. I had the feeling that I had wasted her time. She was right to say that it was a question of temperament, and that I did not have the correct kind. But I no longer believed that equanimity was either tenable or desirable. It corroded everything inside. I had never met a person with greater equanimity than the former president. But this applied to all of them—to the prosecution and the defense, to the judges and even the other interpreters. They were able to work. They had the right temperament for the job. But at what internal cost?

That night, I ventured out to get something to eat, walking to the closest Chinese restaurant. When I entered, the young woman at the register addressed me in Mandarin, her manner hopeful. Her face clouded over when I shook my head and from that point she treated me with greater disdain than seemed normal. I thought—I want to go home. I want to be in a place that feels like home. Where that was, I did not know.

I met Adriaan at a café in his neighborhood. We had been in the habit of going there together and I had been several times while I was still staying in his apartment. But it now felt alien, as if I had returned after a long period of exile. The expectation of his arrival had altered the place. I sat down at a table in the corner of the café, my body so leaden I did not think I would be able to stand again. It had been a week since Adriaan had returned to The Hague, but we had not yet seen each other, we had only spoken on the telephone once, several days earlier.

There had been a brief silence when I answered the phone, and then he said, I'm glad you answered. You left the apartment. His voice was mild, but at the same time it expressed something sharper, and heavier, and I realized then that it had not been without meaning for him, the silence between us. You were gone for longer than I expected, I said. I tried to keep the words from saying too much, but I could not speak of expectation, of what I had once thought to hope, without feeling something yawn open inside. He was very quiet, and then said that it had been complicated in Lisbon, but that he was back, and that it would be best if we could speak in person.

And so we arranged to meet in the café. He arrived not long after I did and I rose to my feet as soon as he came in the door. He crossed the room toward me. I was startled by the physical tumult I experienced in his presence, a feeling that I had almost forgotten. It had been two months since we had last seen each other. We kissed on the cheeks, like mere acquaintances, and then we sat down at the table. He appeared different in some way that I could not immediately identify, as if another version of himself were poking through the familiar exterior.

I saw the news about the trial, he said.

I nodded.

People must be very upset.

I don't think it's the existential threat to the Court that some people are saying it is. But it's not good, no one is happy about it.

Did you ever interpret for him?

I realized again how long he had been gone.

Yes.

What was he like?

He is petty and vain but he understands the depths of human behavior. The places where ordinary people do not go. That gives him a great deal of power, even when he is confined to a cell.

I saw some of the coverage from Lisbon, on the television.

I nodded and looked away. I saw him, in this city I did not know, in an apartment with Gaby and the children, perhaps watching the very journalists I had seen narrate the story of what had taken place. That other life bloomed before my eyes, and the sight of it was more painful than I could have imagined.

I've never been to Lisbon.

It is a beautiful city, he said, as if he could not help but be honest. Very different to this one. Gaby would like the children to stay in Lisbon, but it is difficult. They miss their school here, they have their friends, they cannot simply stay in Portugal because their mother wishes it. At the same time, they need their mother, of course.

Adriaan was hesitating, he did not want to tell me very much more about whatever had taken place in Lisbon, or perhaps he did not know how to put it into words. He looked suddenly tired, and I understood that what had happened had been its own thing for him, in the way that these past months had been for me, and it occurred to me that many years into one possible future, we might be living together in some state of sustained harmony, that against the odds we might yet have succeeded in growing old together. We could be one of those couples whose mutual understanding had such depth and history that we no longer needed to explain things to each other, our routines set long ago, our knowledge of each other, and of our relationship, absolute. And still we might never have told each other what took place these past two months. This time would remain a blind spot in the rearview mirror of our relationship, around which we would carefully maneuver, until the act of that accommodation became second nature, until we no longer even noticed it.

Does that mean that Gaby will remain in Lisbon? I asked. Yes, he said quietly. The children will stay here with me and go to Lisbon during their school holidays. It is not ideal by any stretch of the imagination, I tried very hard to convince Gaby of this fact. But she was adamant. And so I brought the children back with me and we are here once more. In many ways, it is a relief. I am relieved. It is not what I hoped for the children, but I had not realized until I returned to The Hague how much the situation had weighed on me. It is good to have this clarity, however imperfect the outcome.

He paused. I hope you will meet them soon. My children.

I was offered a permanent contract at the Court.

That is wonderful news.

I declined.

I see.

But I saw that he did not see, or that he was not certain

of what the words meant, whether in telling him I had declined the position at the Court I was also telling him that I would no longer be living in The Hague, that I would never meet his children, that there was no possibility of a future between us. I'd had to make the decision without him, I'd had to make it alone. After a moment, he raised his eyes to my face.

Because of the work? Or because of me?

The question was blunt, but I saw that he needed to know, his face was a pure articulation of that need. I looked across the table and at last understood the meaning of what he had just said, that Gaby would be staying in Lisbon and that he had returned to The Hague, that he had come back. It was almost too much to comprehend. Before I could speak he continued.

I'm sorry that I didn't call more often while I was in Portugal. I'm sorry for the long silence. He shook his head. Things were more difficult than I expected. The truth is that I should have been better prepared, after all I was married to Gaby for over fifteen years. But I did not understand how much things between us had deteriorated. He looked at me and lowered his voice. I am sorry about Gaby. I did not know that she intended to go to the apartment, I did not know that she would be in The Hague at all. I would never have inflicted that on you knowingly.

There was a pressure to his voice, to the way he spoke,

and I saw that he understood, or was beginning to understand, how it had been for me those weeks he was away.
And although there were things I had intended to say to
him, words that had passed through my head many times,
words that I had believed needed to be spoken between
us, I said only this: I understand. I could understand anything, under the right circumstances and for the right person. It was both a strength and a weakness. I looked at his
face and I thought it possible that after all, that despite everything, Adriaan was that person for me.

Perhaps you could leave the Court, Adriaan said, but
remain in The Hague?

I reached across the table. He looked down at my hands,
as if they were unfamiliar, or as if he were only now seeing
them again. He grasped them tightly and looked up at me.

I went to the dunes the other day, I said. They're beside
the Court, and yet I had never walked on them. I had never
gone down to the water. It was hard to believe this place
had existed all this time. That this open expanse of sea had
been just outside my field of vision. I looked down, I didn't
know exactly how to proceed, the words seemed to say so
little. Then I learned that I'd been there before, that I'd
spent time here in The Hague with my family as a child.

I fell silent. Perhaps in the end it was not something I
could explain—the prospect that had briefly opened, the
idea that the world might yet be formed or found again. It

was only a simple stretch of sand, the same water that lapped on the shore elsewhere. And yet for a brief moment I had felt the landscape around me vibrate with possibility. I had been trying for so long to put things in their place, to draw a line from one thing to the next.

Should we go there? he asked.

I looked up, startled.

Now?

Yes. It's close. As you know.

I did not reply. Adriaan waved to the waiter, signaling for the bill. I'd been quiet long enough for the silence to take on meaning. I would need to make a decision. Yes, I said softly. He turned around and I saw that in his eyes there was nonetheless a glimmer of hope. That we might yet proceed from here. That this might yet be enough. He reached for my hand, his face turned toward me. And so I said it again. I said yes.

ACKNOWLEDGMENTS

I am immensely grateful to the Public Affairs Unit of the International Criminal Court in The Hague, and to interpreters Ahmed El Khamloussy and Andrew Constable for sharing their insight and expertise. Thank you also to Hunter Braithwaite for his invaluable research and forensic mind. Although the court that appears in this novel shares certain similarities with the International Criminal Court, it is in no way intended to represent that institution or its activities.

Thank you to Ellen Levine, Laura Perciasepe, Jynne Dilling Martin, Claire McGinnis, Clare Conville, Michal Shavit, Ana Fletcher, and the remarkable teams at Riverhead and Jonathan Cape. Thank you also to Deborah Landau and the community at the Writers House. Large parts of this novel were written at the Santa Maddalena Foundation, and I am grateful to Beatrice Monti, Andrew Sean Greer, and Andrea Bajani for their kindness and support.

Finally, thank you as ever and always, to Hari.